INVADED BY VIDEOGAMES

METAVERSE LEGENDS
BOOK 3

JUSTIN M. STONE

————

Our siblings' fight to stop Simon and find their dad brings them to a new adventure... this time right here in the real world.

Although many challenges lie ahead, Lucas and his friends are more determined than ever to prevent other evil forces from threatening humanity. Using their newfound powers, together they track down the source of Simon's latest evil plan—bringing monsters in from the metaverse to attack Earth!

And this time their fight takes them to Tokyo, Japan!

Before their mission is over, they'll find that not all monsters come in the form of, well, monsters. With new allies and more foreboding enemies in the mix, it's more important than ever that these siblings and their friends learn to work as a team.

If they don't, life on Earth will never be the same.

1

LUCAS

Thin rays of light from the streetlamp outside shone through the blinds of Lucas's bedroom, casting a glare on his TV as he tried to play an old-school version of Zelda. Lucas wanted a break from all the virtual and augmented reality he had experienced lately, especially since the virtual world he'd been in had been real.

Playing games was a way to take his mind off the matter. He was supposed to be asleep, but with all his worrying lately, that didn't mean much. At least they hadn't had to move to Arizona yet. Judging by the way his mom kept worrying about it, that day was coming soon—as soon as their aunt was ready for them. The longer she could delay it, the better, as far as Lucas was concerned.

He had just acquired a new boomerang in the game when his door flew open. His sister, Madison, came charging into his room. She had changed her hair to match her avatar from the other worlds. Bright pink streaks ran through her otherwise black hair like warpaint, and the pink extended down to her jawline. Compared to his own blond, she had become the more eccentric of the two.

"Put down the controller right now," Madison said.

Lucas did no such thing. "If it's not an emergency, don't interrupt my gameplay."

It wasn't entirely her fault he was annoyed. No, if he thought about it, he knew his irritation was because Jacob had been too busy to hang out since they had defeated Simon. Maybe it was that Jacob wanted to forget all about the craziness they'd gone through, or maybe it was more about him finally uncovering the side of himself that enjoyed being competitive. But every day, Jacob had been out practicing to join the baseball team. At least the boy probably had a much stronger swing now that they had practiced so much with a battleax.

Madison stared at Lucas, waiting. He finally set down his controller, slowly turned to her, then folded his arms across his chest. He then noticed the stench in his room that likely came from the plate of unfinished fries and gravy in the corner.

"This is an emergency," Madison said. "I just can't stop thinking about it, the U and S…"

"I get it," Lucas said. "You want it to be something. You want to believe the ski lodge in the other world was somehow related to Dad—maybe a sign that he's still around—but I think you're grasping at straws."

"Grasping at straws?"

"You know what I mean. It's a stretch… You know, like trying to grab water."

"Grabbing water is easy. All you have to do is cup your hands." Madison demonstrated with imaginary water. "See?"

"You missed the point. Simon is gone. All that craziness is over. Ralli is safe and her world isn't in danger anymore. Can't we just be happy with that and do what we do best?"

"Even Ralli said we might be going back, or seeing her or whatever, sooner than we expect. Don't we owe it to dad and mom to try and find him?"

Lucas turned back and picked up his controller but didn't press start. He was too busy gripping the controller as if he was going to break it in two. How could Madison even start to think that he wouldn't be as devoted to finding their dad as she was? Lucas wanted to throw the controller across the room, to stand up and turn on her and shout. Instead, he just stared at the screen.

"Why don't you just try again," Madison finally said, breaking the silence.

"It doesn't work."

"It hasn't worked yet. That doesn't mean it will never work. Give me the headset. Lemme try. Maybe Ralli wasn't listening before. Maybe she'll be waiting this time, call us back to that world and..."

"Dad's not there, as much as we both want him to be. The two of us need to stop dreaming. It's time we accept that we're back in reality now."

"You're talking like you don't even believe it ever happened."

"No, we've been through that before. Of course I know it happened. But I also know when it's over, it's over. If Simon was going to do anything, if he's even still around, don't you think it would've happened by now? My guess is, he got lost in the metaverse, and maybe we'll see his face pop up on some TV screen someday as a digital version of himself begging to be let out. We'll just turn off the TV and walk away and never see him again."

Madison let out an annoyed grunt as she went to his closet to open the top drawer where the headset was kept. "I don't care what you say, I'm trying."

There wasn't much he could do. It wasn't like he was going to fight her to try and make her stop. It didn't matter because, as he watched, the same thing happened that had happened every other time – she put on the headset, booted up again, and started calling for Ralli to help.

"Bring us back to your world," Madison said. "Ralli, I know you're there. Please... be there."

That way she asked for help brought back awful memories. It was too quiet in his bedroom, too muted from the sounds of Zelda. He turned off the game and then the TV.

Ralli was gone, which meant it was time he stopped living in a fantasy world and accepted that they were back here on Earth. He and his sister were trying to figure out what they were going to do next with themselves.

Madison waited for a response, called out a few more times, and then placed the headset on the desk and looked over at Lucas with defeat in her eyes. He gave her a half-hearted shrug as if to say he told her so. Inside he was just as disappointed as she was.

"What should we do?" she asked. "We can't search for Dad with what little clues we have left forever. I don't know if this was some kind of test to see if we're ready to know or not ready, or maybe just to see if we really do care. All I know is that Dad is still out there somewhere and we have to find him."

"Dad's gone," Lucas said. And not wanting to deal with the judgment and sorrow in her eyes, he turned away from her.

Instead of responding, Lucas pulled out his phone and started looking over Java and Python coding videos on YouTube. He had recently been inspired to follow the path of his dad, to become a developer. While his older sister turned to hopeless dreams of finding their dad, Lucas opted instead for this connection. He had even started to get a basic understanding of programming and begun playing around with blueprints and other game development tools.

A clearing of Madison's throat told him she wasn't going to let this be, so he set down the phone. No matter how much he tried to think of something to say to comfort her, he couldn't.

"I'm going for a walk," Lucas finally said, his

voice breaking. He didn't care that it was a Saturday and that they were supposed to spend the day together. The only thing he could think about was how frustrated he was with the whole situation and how nothing he could say would change things.

He was only halfway out the door when his sister darted out after him.

"There's a call," Madison said, nearly out of breath. "It's... from India."

Lucas turned to her and saw the phone held out, the name Sarika there on the display. Lucas took a step back toward his sister, then hesitated. His heart thudded as he wondered why Sarika would be calling him. They had met on the other side in the metaverse. Never once had they spoken in the real world, but using their connection through Ralli, he had been able to tell her his phone number and address in case she wanted to get in touch with him. For a second, he wondered if she was in the area and if she just wanted to meet at the park or go to the mall or something. Dread came over him. His mind started racing with other reasons she might be calling. Finally, unable to take it anymore, he took the phone and slowly lifted it to his ear.

"This is Lucas..."

"Took you long enough." The voice on the other

end of the line was distant, barely recognizable. He'd never spoken with her on the phone, so he figured this was likely something to do with being a long-distance call. "Did your sister tell you what's up?"

"No..." He looked over to see that Madison already had her laptop open at the dining room table.

She was turning around to show him the video. It said live stream, but that didn't look right. Despite showing an older temple with Japanese people nearby, a bright light had formed in the sky. It was purple with a black outline. A pixilated monster seemed to be emerging from it! This had to be some-body playing a trick. Maybe some Photoshop skills on display? He would've believed that if not for the fact that they were all waiting and expecting a move on Simon's part.

"What are we going to do?" Madison asked.

"It's time to get the team back together," Sarika said. "We have to stop this."

Lucas put the phone on speaker and set it down next to the laptop as he leaned over to stare at the incoming monster. It was massive with eight legs like a spider, but parts of it gleamed black like metal. And at its head was, instead of a face or spider eyes, the torso of a man. The man had no face, as the black metal covered his entire body and head.

A chill ran through Lucas, and his eyes met his sister's. Hers didn't hold the fear that he felt rising up inside him, instead gleaming with excitement.

"Oh boy," she said. "It's on like a crouton. We're going to Tokyo!"

2

MADISON

As she stared at her brother, excitement burst out of her. She stood and started pacing, already planning all the cool stuff they would do if they really did get to Tokyo.

"Did you know they built a Studio Ghibli Museum there?" she asked. "I say we go there first, then we go to this place called the Ramen Museum that shows all the different ways noodle dishes are made. If we get a chance, the food will help our training. Oooh, then we visit the Nikko temples. I can't wait to try all the—"

"Whoa, whoa, whoa." Lucas held his hands up, waving them. "Hello, we are going there to stop Simon from bringing his monsters into our world from the metaverse. Did you forget about that little fact? I mean I don't think we will have time to go sightseeing. Unless he's attacking Mount Fuji, we're not going there either. All that sounds great, but let's go back a step. How would we possibly get to Tokyo to begin with? Japan is on the other side of the world!"

Madison turned on her brother, arguments forming in her mind. First she was going to say that she didn't mean right away. This was all after they defeated Simon. But he had a good point. Regardless of everything she wanted to do in Japan, they didn't have any way of figuring out how to get there to begin with.

"Okay, how do we get there." She sat on his bed, fingers steepled beneath her chin as she thought. "Without money, we can't buy a ticket. Even if we could, it would take too long."

"How long would it take," Lucas asked.

"Doesn't matter, but I think about twelve hours."

"Right. We need to get there now. So all we have to do is break the laws of physics, and..."

"What?"

"That's just it. We don't care about the laws of physics. I mean, we went into a videogame. We did all kinds of crazy stuff in there, and if somehow

Simon has found a way to bring creatures from that world to ours, shouldn't we be able to do the same?"

"You want to try and summon a monster?"

"No, not summon a monster, but summon someone we know." He was smiling all goofy, so she knew he had something exciting on his mind. Then it hit her.

"Instead of just trying to contact Ralli, you want to bring her here."

"Bring her here, and she can help us figure out how we get to Tokyo. To stop that."

Both looked at the screen again, and Madison's heart thudded in her chest. The crazy-looking spider creature had fully emerged and was descending on a long thread to the top of the Tokyo Tower. The massive metal structure stood tall against the back-drop of a sunrise, orange standing out against the grey skyscrapers surrounding it.

Crowds were lined around the tower with their phones out to take pictures. None of them were looking at the beauty of the glowing sunlight as it sparkled on the metal of the tower. Not with that spider-creature incoming.

"And you have a plan for this?" Madison asked.

"We still have the key, right? Since that's what

Simon wanted above all else, I assume it can also prove useful in this situation."

"Good thinking. Let's make it happen."

The two huddled around Lucas's computer, and Madison pulled out the key. They weren't sure what to do exactly, so Madison relied on instinct. Simon had been after this thing for a reason and had thrown practically all he had at trying to retrieve it. Knowing the key had a connection to the other worlds, or was the connective tissue of all worlds—the metaverse—she simply focused on Ralli and willed her to come to them.

A bright light flickered between them, expanding. With a flash, it expanded and then was gone. Ralli stood there, looking at them with surprise. She wore a black shirt that showed off her midsection along with brown pants, a gold belt buckle, and a side holster for a blaster. Her black hair was long and pulled into a ponytail—no longer frizzy as it had been when they first met her. A wide smile spread across her face.

Ralli took a deep breath and then coughed. "Your world stinks!" She laughed and then gave them both a hug. "What's going on? How... Why?"

Madison quickly explained what was going on, how they had seen the monster come through, and how the only explanation could be that Simon was behind it.

"We defeated him in the metaverse," Ralli said with a heavy sigh. "But I always knew that wouldn't be the end of him. On my side, I was preparing defenses in case Simon returned. Apparently, he had something else in mind."

"So, how do we stop him?" Madison asked.

"Just like you summoned me here, I think we're going to have to travel via the metaverse. We re-upload ourselves, follow a digital trail, and exit when the time is right." Ralli beamed as if that made sense.

Since Lucas was nodding and smiling, Madison did the same. The two of them could figure it out together, and she would go along for the ride.

"And your friends?" Ralli asked.

"Of course," Lucas replied. He already had his phone out to text Jacob.

Madison did the same with Sarika, letting her know they had found a way. "We'll pick you up along the way."

"Pick me up?" Sarika asked.

"Just pinging your computer and sending a screenshot so we have each other's locations. It seems we don't need the VR headsets for this like when we went into the game—not when we have the key."

Ralli glanced over as she whispered, "You might not want to go around saying you have the key. If anyone is listening, digitally or in person, that could put us in trouble."

Madison shared a look with her brother and then gave their friend a subtle nod. She reached into her pocket before holding out the key. Although they hadn't had much experience with this yet, she knew what needed to be done. This thing gave them the power to traverse the metaverse, so she hoped this would work.

Taking her brother's hand in hers, Madison checked the screenshot as it came in. From what she could tell, this took a lot of energy out of her, so she would have to get it right. As long as she was near a computer and knew where to target, the key would allow them to travel.

Her brother had Jacob ready to go, so Madison directed the key toward the computer, focused, and then made it happen. What followed was a series of pixels swarming around them, bright lights, and then a flash like lightning.

The next thing they knew, the light was fading and Madison found herself kneeling on cement. She raised her eyes to see a dog statue and Ralli at her side, with a small line of trees or past the statue and then skyscrapers in a mesh of glass and bright colors.

"Did we make it?" Madison asked. "Where are the boys? They came through, and I..."

Before she could finish the sentence, a grunt sounded from behind a small, raised area of trees and flowers. She ran around it to see Lucas helping Jacob off the ground, the latter staring past both of them to the skyscrapers above.

"Where are we?" Jacob asked.

Tall buildings. A train station... but no people. No noise. The place was eerily empty and dead quiet! Never in the pictures or movies of this place had it been so empty. The buildings were strange and overwhelming. They had large screens showing intricate Japanese characters, like an animated billboard.

The three stood frozen in the middle of a wide intersection, the skyscrapers towering over them like warrior guards with columns lined up as far as the eye could see, fading back into the sky where dark clouds began to roll in from the horizon. On the street, cars were abandoned, some on their sides with smashed windows.

No bodies... only that silence. Madison had never experienced that quiet before – like everything was hushed and resting.

"This is Tokyo!" Lucas said. "I recognize it from that *Ghostwire* game."

"I thought Mom told you not to play that one," Madison chided him.

He gestured around as if to ask whether playing the games he wasn't supposed to play mattered, considering their circumstances. Good point. The air held a stale odor, like a laundry room when the dryer had been going too long.

"Not bad," Jacob said, his eyes wide.

Lucas glanced his way, hesitantly replying, "Not bad for our first hang out in... how long?"

"Dude, you know I've been busy with baseball practice and all that. It wasn't personal."

Lucas arched a brow, clearly doubting that, but then sniffed, glancing around.

"I taste smoke in the air," Ralli said, noticing as well, "like something's burning."

Madison lifted her head, sniffing. She didn't smell anything like that. More like... metallic? A clanging broke through the silence, followed by a scream.

"This way!" Madison said, then sprinted to an

alley across the street.

They darted past vending machines for dispensing teas and coffees right alongside sodas. Some even had shoes and socks. Emerging onto a street that overlooked an underpass, they saw a line of cherry blossom trees in full bloom on the opposite side. That's where they found what they were looking for. A dark creature vanished through a broken wall on the balcony of a building above.

"After it," Madison said, muscles clenched as she prepared to sprint. A hand gripped her wrist and spun her around.

"That monster we saw?" Jacob eyed her and then the others. "We're just kids. How are we supposed to do anything against that?"

"You kidding?" Ralli scoffed. "After all we've been through?"

"But I mean, that was in the game world."

Madison scoffed, though a moment of doubt hit her. She held out her hand, hoping she was right about what she was expecting. Sure enough, her massive, glowing sword materialized into her hand.

"How...?" Jacob asked.

"Since we went through the metaverse to get here, we have a connection still," she answered.

"Close enough," Ralli interjected. "Actually, since

you have the key and my connection, we should be able to summon more. For example..."

With a nod, she created a small portal through which their creature friends Fido and Easter came stumbling out of.

"Wha—where are we?" Easter asked. This large lizard creature had wings and a grin, and while not equipped with them at the moment, would be able to summon a bow and arrow when needed.

Fido was, surprisingly, still mostly in dog form.

"No time," Madison replied, and was back to running over to where they had spotted the creature vanishing into the building.

Except, there was no need. As soon as she stepped into the area where light streamed between the tall buildings, another movement caught her attention. This time, it was from her right, and she spun to see a massive furball with a wide mouth and long claws. Her first thought was that it reminded her of Totoro from one of those Japanese movies Lucas so loved. Except, when it leaped over and consumed him, she knew it was nothing like the sweet protector from the movie.

This monster had just consumed her brother!

3

LUCAS

Lucas had been about to summon his sword, but then a shadow enveloped him. He was surrounded by complete darkness. He tried to move, confused, only to find himself bouncing around inside of something soft.

A dark bounce house, maybe? No, that didn't make sense. He tried to reach out and summon his sword in case there was trouble. Before he could, he was flung forward again, unable to do the summoning.

"Hello?!" he shouted, his stomach lurching and bile in his mouth. If this kept up, he had no doubt his last meal would soon be splattered everywhere in whatever this dark bounce house was.

This went on for what seemed an eternity. His

fears got the best of him as he imagined himself dying – or worse, being handed over to Simon. He could already see it, him wearing a mind-control helmet and serving that jerk against his will. Trying again and again to get his mind clear, Lucas finally started to focus on the immediate here and now. Whatever was happening, he needed to find an escape. More than that, he needed to find a way to get back to his sister and friends.

Maybe he couldn't escape on his own, but could at least send them a signal of where he was? After all, he had come through the metaverse and was still connected. They should be able to trace him!

Focusing his mental energy on connecting in that way, he saw pixelated light float around, giving him a brief glimpse of the inside of the creature that had swallowed him.

Words appeared that said, "Trace finished" before vanishing.

He held his breath, hoping that would do the trick. To his relief, muffled sounds came from nearby. A glimpse of light came from above—the mouth of whatever he was inside of opening?—and movement again. He was jostled about, dazed and confused, and again felt his stomach threatening to spew out its contents.

Something connected and caused his dark prison to contract so that the pressure of the strike hit him as well with a thud upside the head.

"*Ow!*" Lucas shouted.

"Lucas?" a voice asked, and then more strikes came, harder and with increased ferocity.

"Stop—ooomph—hitting—oomph—me!"

"Sorry, it's just..."

That light appeared again, followed by an arm reaching in. After jamming a large stick in place to keep the mouth open, Sarika's face appeared.

"Let's get you out of here," she said, reaching in with both hands.

Lucas took her hands. As soon as he was free of the creature, his lunch spewed out onto the grass. At least none of it hit Sarika! Speaking of her, he looked up, wiped his mouth, and said, "Where'd you come from?"

"Ralli sent me," Sarika said with a slight accent that he placed from India. She looked like she had when he met her in the metaverse, except now she wore baggy, beige pants and a cute pink shirt. Plus, she was, as she had suggested when they'd last seen each other, in a wheelchair.

"And my sister? Jacob?"

"A bit occupied, by my understanding." Sarika

motioned behind her, where her hover snowboard was stowed in the back of her wheelchair. "Wasn't about to leave this in the other world. Coming?"

"You bet." She made a motion so that the snowboard appeared beneath her wheels, locking her in place. It was like the snowboard had been made for this, and as it hovered up and off the ground, she held out a hand to help him up.

Once he was steady and had his hand still in hers—gulp!—he asked, "Where to?"

"That monster was trying to deliver you to Simon," Sarika replied. "Ralli retrieved me and sent me after you, but looking at this map here..."

She held up an arm where a watch displayed a holographic image of streets and had the Japanese signal for Tokyo on it. Lucas knew that much just from video games.

"What are we looking for?" he asked.

A red blip showed up as if in answer. Sarika navigated the snowboard through more overturned cars and even destroyed buildings.

"We think that's the building Simon's operating out of. Carrot Tower, Sangenjaya," she said.

"You speak Japanese?"

"Studied it for a bit, yeah. I was actually going to a tech school back home, preparing for a research internship in Japan, so... this all sort of worked out perfectly, huh?"

Lucas scoffed. "If you call a crazy billionaire summoning monsters from the metaverse to destroy a city perfect, then yeah, sure."

"Agh, you know what I mean."

He wasn't sure he did. Except, as he remembered that his arms were wrapped around her and they were together again, he thought maybe she was right. While this was scary, at least the situation was bringing all of them together again. Or together once they managed to meet back up, anyway. At the moment, he was separated from Madison, Ralli, and Jacob.

They flew through side streets, passing areas that clearly had no idea what was going on. One street was full of young boys and girls in black school uniforms, the girls in skirts, and they all turned and made sounds of surprise and excitement. At the next street, others were running toward the previous one, screams telling Lucas that this group knew what was coming. More than that, their screams told him he and Sarika were going in the right direction.

"Get ready," Sarika said.

"This isn't the game world," Lucas said. "Are we going to be able to fight those monsters?"

"Dude." She grinned as she held out one of her hands in front of them. In a flash of pink and blue pixels, a blaster pistol appeared in her hand. "We're gonna have some fun."

Her excitement inspired him. Keeping one arm on her wheelchair to not fall off the flying snowboard, he held out his other and summoned his sword.

"Not bad," she said, and then summoned a curved blade in her free hand. "I wouldn't say it's as cool as my Tulwar blade, but to each their own."

"Tulwar? You named it?"

She laughed. "No, no. It's a type of sword from India—curved like this. Figured it was more fun to have that cultural heritage than the game one I'd used before."

"Oh, that's pretty cool and—"

"Jump!" she interrupted.

"What?"

"You heard me."

Without another word, Sarika's wheelchair went rolling forward and straight off the snowboard. She had her blaster up and shot as she went flying into the air and headed straight for that monster.

"No, no, no," Lucas said as the snowboard started to twist and shake out of control.

He braced himself for pain as he threw himself out into the air with his sword held in both hands. As before, darkness surrounded him. This time he was ready. Spinning in the air and thrusting with his sword, he stabbed. The blade hit and he felt himself jerked over and then down as the monster's flesh resisted. Next thing he knew, he was sliding down, cutting the creature so that it pixelated back to its own dimension as he landed on the ground.

He turned to see an amazing sight—as Sarika landed, her wheelchair had transformed into exoskeleton-like leg supports. She was fighting and moving about and jumping and kicking with extra strength!

Screeching filled the air, and he turned to see flying creatures that reminded him of hairy dinosaurs with wings. He immediately called upon the lava function of his sword. As bursts of red shot out and pixelated the monsters to vanish, he collapsed to his knees with exhaustion. His XP shot up. One more monster came at him, but this one was almost cute. Like a cuddly ball with long legs, it skipped along with its lips pursed together, whistling. Suddenly it turned on him, lips spreading to form a wide mouth with sharp teeth, and then it lunged. With his final burst of energy, he thrust out his sword and cut it in two so that it pixelated out of existence with an increase in his XP.

Lucas collapsed to the ground. He stared up at the flowing clouds overhead as he tried to place the tune that the monster had been whistling. Had it been a Christmas carol? He shook his head, almost laughing at the idea.

A shadow blocked his view. He would have attacked but had no energy to do so. As his eyes adjusted, he saw Sarika standing over him, pistol and pirate blade at her hips. She stepped aside and turned to look at a tall, orange building.

"There it is—Carrot Tower," she said. "And Simon."

Considering the dark cloud circling around the top of the orange brick building, she had to be correct. This was one hundred percent Simon's doing.

"That's... awesome," he said, eyeing her exoskeleton leg supports. "How..."

She grinned. "A level upgrade. Just tried it out since I had an extra skill point. Glad you like 'em, but it's exhausting. I'll switch back and forth as needed." With that, she let them transform back to the wheelchair and let out a sigh of relief. "I'm more used to this."

Lucas gave her a nod before assessing the tower. "How do we get inside?"

"For that, I think we're going to need some help." With a sly grin, Sarika held up her watch and said, "Connect to Ralli."

4

MADISON

"I still can't believe he's gone," Madison said, trying to get the image out of her head of that monster running off after it had swallowed her brother.

Ralli knelt next to her, a hand on her shoulder. "Sarika is strong and knows what she's doing. She'll find him. Now get up so we can finish this, yeah?"

Madison turned from her to see Jacob standing, his massive battle ax at the ready, anxious for the fight that awaited them through those doors. They had pursued the dark shape from before to this point, and roaring and shouting came from the other side of that door.

"Let's do it," Madison said, then strolled over to the door.

"Wait, shouldn't you call upon your friends?" Ralli asked.

"My brother? That's why we're..."

"No, I mean the little animals... Fido and Easter —where'd they run off to?"

Jacob yelped. "They were swallowed by something, too. I saw it, but it vanished in the chaos..." His eyes were wide and full of worry.

"I got this," Madison said. Using the key as she had before, she summoned them. A flash of light went off and left Fido and Easter standing there in front of her.

"Whoa, yuck," Fido said, shaking himself dry of yuck and goo. "We tried to go after Lucas but were swallowed by another monster."

Easter scrunched up her dragon nose and spat something green. "It was disgusting."

"It's about time!" Easter said. "I was growing worried about you."

Jacob ran forward and threw his arms around Fido. Since the creature was still in dog form, it wagged its tail and panted excitedly.

"Don't ever scare me like that again," Jacob said.

Fido frowned. "Give me more powers, and maybe I won't get eaten. I honestly don't know what Easter's excuse is."

Easter looked like she was about to hit the dog-like creature, but that was interrupted by a hug from Madison. After a lizard tongue darted out in surprise, the silly lizard returned the hug. With all the upgrades Madison had given her, the lizard looked more like a dog-sized dragon. Both could talk, and both had at one point been creations of Simon's but had proven themselves in their last adventure and the fight against him.

"We still have to get to Tokyo Tower," Ralli said. "Get there, fight that monster, and hope Lucas finds his way to us."

Madison ignored the lump in her throat, pushing back the emotions and worry over her brother. "He knew that was the destination, after all."

"He's going to be okay," Jacob said, hand on his ax, turning it as if eager for the next fight.

"I know." Madison forced a hopeful smile as she pointed to the tip of orange metal visible through buildings ahead. "There she is, ladies and gents."

Without another moment's hesitation, they charged up the stairs and cement walkway that led to their destination. Madison turned to look at a vending machine, intrigued to see that it sold sandwiches and balls of seaweed and rice. She was about to kick herself for the distraction, but she saw movement in the reflection.

Spinning, Madison found herself watching as part of a building crumbled away and into a tunnel.

"What's...?" Jacob asked, coming back to stand at her side.

Madison, Ralli, and Jacob stood frozen as the monster worms emerged from the tunnel. The creatures were easily twice the size of a human. Their sickly green skin was covered in writhing tentacles.

"What do we do?" Ralli whispered, her voice shaking with fear.

"We fight," Madison said firmly, her eyes narrowing as she readied her large sword. Her hand went to her head and she grinned at finding her goggles that she'd been equipped with in the other world. "These things aren't going to take us down without a fight."

At her side, Easter rose into the sky with bow and arrow ready. Jacob nodded, ax held high with two hands. Fido growled nearby. Ralli leaped over, covering more ground than would have made sense if she wasn't from another world.

"Can't we ever just get to our destination without monsters getting into our way?" She summoned a magic staff, gave it a look, and then shook it so that it transformed into a large, pink-and-black war hammer.

"Awesome!" Jacob said.

"You know it." She lifted the war hammer and sent a pink blast of energy at the worms.

The closest worm fell back, shaking from the blast, but the rest lunged forward, their sharp teeth glinting with light.

Without hesitation, the three kids and the pets charged at the worms, shouting and brandishing their weapons. The worms writhed and twisted as they were struck, but they didn't seem to be deterred. They kept coming, their mouths snapping and their tentacles flailing.

Madison knew they needed to conserve their energy, so she glanced around and saw what she was looking for—a narrow alleyway.

"That way," she said, indicating with her sword before turning back to slice through a worm. "Get them so they can't all attack at once."

"Go!" Ralli said, but as they started back toward it, she pointed out. "Of course, they could come at us from below."

The girl leaped forward, hammer up and surging with pink light as she charged it. She landed and brought the hammer down hard so that a bright flash of light filled the air, causing nearby worms to disintegrate.

Madison laughed and said, "Why didn't you do that to begin with!"

Another tunnel opened next to her, and she spun with a thrust into the opening, the glow showing the worm for a split second before it pixelated away from Earth. Her screen showed a good twenty XP added. What leveling up in the real world might mean was beyond her understanding. Right now, she had to focus.

"They'll keep coming," Ralli said, indicating the road ahead. "Get to the tower!"

"Agreed," Jacob shouted as he charged ahead with Fido.

Dodging pedestrians and weaving through traffic, they made their way through the bustling city, their feet pounding against the pavement. They crested a hill to see Tokyo Tower looming ahead, its bright white and orange exterior standing out against the skyline. As they neared the tower, Madison's excitement rose along with her anxiety. Where was Lucas? She hoped he had found a way to escape and would be waiting for them at the tower.

When they reached the base, however, there was no sign of him. Panting and out of breath, they looked up at the towering structure and then to each other.

"We made it!" Ralli exclaimed, grinning widely.

"And we're just in time," Jacob added, indicating a position three-quarters of the way up. Madison leaned back and gulped at the sight of purple and black spiderwebs with a series of people caught up in the webs.

Glaring down at them was that nasty, metallic spider creature they had seen on the computer. It made a clicking noise and then shot out one of those black lengths of webbing. Madison pulled Jacob aside so that it hit the ground beside him. A purple burst of light lit it up. Both had to dive to avoid getting hit.

Recovering, the kids looked at each other and nodded, their determination renewed. They had come this far. They wouldn't let anything stop them from making their stand against Simon at the top of Tokyo Tower. Taking a deep breath, they started toward the entrance, prepared to climb and make their attack on the spider creature.

"Don't stop, no matter what," Madison said.

Ralli grinned. "To the top!"

As a group, they charged up the stairs. On the next flight, lights flickered and then turned off. The glow from their weapons was all they had to go off of for sight. Clicking sounded, followed by mini spiders appearing in their path.

Jacob was in the lead and brought his ax down on one but missed. The spider leaped up onto his back and bit, causing him to scream. Madison wasn't sure her powers from the other worlds would all work here, but she went on instinct. With a blast from her sword, she shot the spider from Jacob. It went flying and landed with the rest of the spiders. Each were about a foot tall, all clanking and made of metal.

"Work smart," Ralli said, hammer ready.

Madison eyed the stairwell, seeing that it was narrow and wouldn't fit more than one person fighting at a time. The spiders had the advantage due to their smaller size.

"I got this," she said before sending out a shock wave at the spiders. Three of them moved up the sides of the walls. One jumped for her and connected, followed by another. She felt their bites, followed by numbness and inability to move.

"That wasn't smart!" Ralli chided. She slammed the wall with her hammer to send a blast of pink electricity along it. The two spiders still there fell, twitching. Jacob was as frozen in place as Madison, but Easter shot one of the spiders already damaged, and the arrow took it out as Fido charged around, barking.

A touch from Ralli made the numbness vanish, and then she realized how this worked. Spiders were converging on Jacob, but he was immobilized. They weren't just going to sting him. They were going for the kill!

But Madison had an idea. She charged directly into their path and shoved Jacob back and down the stairs in hopes of Ralli stopping his fall. She took a deep breath, preparing herself. The spiders were almost on her, but she waited until the exact right moment.

Three, two... one.

As the creatures leaped through the air, one's leg brushing against her cheek, and she performed her Shadow Move. It would take one-third of her mana, and she was already down some from her last blast. She would need some left over for the massive spider at the top, and of course Simon, but she didn't see any other way here.

Her Shadow Blast made her vanish from her location and reappear just past the last spider, on the ledge above. An added bonus of her Shadow Move was the small explosion it left behind, and that was enough to knock the spiders back to slam into the walls and stairs.

"Now!" she said, spinning to slice at the closest spider.

Ralli had Jacob, helping him to stand, and both turned with surprise to see her on the ledge. They leaped into action in a game like Whack-a-Mole, taking those spiders out before they could attack again.

Easter shot at one nearby, and Madison kicked it to send it flying off the tower. One more was at her feet, so she lifted her sword and brought it down to slam into the largest spider. It pixelated out and then was gone. In a flurry of attacks and bursts of light, they cleared out the rest of the creatures.

Madison's XP rose by 50 for each spider that she had directly destroyed. Three of them meant 150 XP. Not bad, though she wondered how it could matter, this being Earth. Her skills were working, as odd as that was.

"That won't be the end of it," Ralli said. "Stay close, and—"

A beep from Ralli's wrist sounded, followed by a voice.

"Madi, is that you?"

It was Lucas! Madison turned to Ralli with

confusion. The girl grinned and held out a hand with glowing wires just under the skin. It projected an image that showed Lucas with an Indian girl in a wheelchair that had to be Sarika.

"Lucas?" Madison asked, taking Ralli's wrist so she could hold the image in front of her face. Without a doubt, this was her brother—not dead! "How dare you get eaten like that? Tell me where you are right now!"

"We're at Carrot Tower, and something's definitely up here."

"It's got to be another entry point for his monsters," Ralli said. "He's using specific locations as portals to bring over his followers from the metaverse."

"So we destroy those zones and save the day?" Lucas asked through the holo screen.

"No, that wouldn't do it." Ralli swiped her hand through the air, bringing the maps and screens to float in front of her. Waving a hand through them, she made the rest disappear except for three glowing dots. "He's triangulated his connection. If we could readjust the signal, focus it to a location of our choosing..."

"Bring the fight to us?" Madison asked.

Ralli nodded. "We make them fight on our terms long enough to break the signal. That should do it."

"And this tower?" Sarika asked, squeezing in close to Lucas to ensure she was visible, even though that wasn't necessary.

"Leave it, we have to focus our efforts on one location, and we don't have the power to—"

"No, don't," a new voice sounded.

Madison shared a confused look with Ralli, but the image was interrupted by digital lines briefly before a new face appeared. This was a boy of about sixteen, Japanese, his hair plastered down with sweat.

"My name is Aki, and I'm in Tokyo Tower, fighting these monsters," the boy said. "I only picked up your signal because I was trying to reach my contact to fight these things. If you can find my buddy and help us secure Tokyo Tower, I believe we could hold it while you all get to Carrot Tower."

"Not bad thinking!" Ralli said. "If we can hold two of the three locations, our chances of success will be that much better."

"Like a Headquarters Mode in an FPS," Jacob said, grinning widely.

"What?" Madison asked.

"Trust me."

"Could be a trap," Ralli pointed out. "But... I met Aki on the other side. He seemed to be one of the few good ones."

"Then we go and hope it's not a trap, but be ready in case it is," Lucas said. "We do what we can for the boy until we know for sure."

Sarika gave a nod at his side and said, "We'll try to take Tokyo Tower and have it ready for you all when you're done there."

"Couldn't you hide and wait for us?" Madison asked.

"There might not be time," Lucas replied. "Plus, with the number of monsters already here, I'm sure they'd find us. Better to continue the charge."

"Fine, but be carefu—"

Before she could finish the sentence, the signal cut out. Madison frowned, finally released Ralli's wrist, and nodded. "Let's hurry this up to get to Carrot Tower ASAP."

With that, they continued their ascent up Tokyo Tower, the spider monster making screeching noises and filling them with dread. Not that a little fright could stop them.

5

LUCAS

Staring up at the orange bricks of the building known as Carrot Tower, Lucas had to wonder what it would have been like to come here under different circumstances. To stroll up, grab a strange drink from the vending machine, and then take the elevator to the top for a nice view of the city. Instead, he held his lava sword with clammy hands, chest rising and falling rapidly, and watched as the dark clouds above descended upon them while fog crept in from all the surrounding streets.

"This is... creeping me out," he admitted. "Have you ever, I mean..."

"Done anything like this?" She laughed. "I was having fun in what I thought was a game back there with Stryka and the others, and next thing I know it turns out to be real... So no, other than that last fight we all had where I finally joined you, this would be a first for me."

"Same here."

He wanted to kick himself, feeling silly about how he was handling this. At least he wasn't the only one not sure how to handle the situation.

An old woman rode by on her bike, turning to look at them with confusion. Nearby fog was almost on her. Lucas thought nothing of it until he saw a dark shape move in the fog—like a tentacle. Before she had completely vanished in the fog, she suddenly moved fast and to the side as if yanked out of sight.

Lucas gulped.

"Something tells me we don't want to go into that fog," he said.

Sarika's blaster was shaking in her hand. "I couldn't agree with you more. And since it's getting closer to us..."

"We should move."

Neither of them budged, both as scared of what was in the building as in that fog. Pushing aside all hesitation, Lucas finally stepped toward the door, sword ready.

"At least in there we can likely see what we're fighting," he said. "Not so much out here."

That was enough to convince her, and together they entered. Neither wanted to say that they had no idea how Ralli and the others would find their way to join up, considering the fog. If Ralli had shown them one thing, though, it was that she was resilient and always found a way.

Without further hesitation... they entered through the glass doors with "Tokyo" written above them.

The lobby inside was surprisingly unassuming but lit in a warm, natural color. Lucas stepped forward, followed by Sarika as she transformed her wheelchair into exoskeleton legs. He froze at strange thudding from within. Something large was moving below.

"What is that noise?" he whispered to her, head swiveling back and forth as if expecting to see some giant monster or ghost appear at any moment.

Sarika stared ahead, wide-eyed, holding her blaster out before her.

"I don't know," she said breathlessly.

She seemed to have been completely thrown off by the loudness of the room. The elevator directly across from them gave off a gentle tone in warning—chimed once, twice, then it opened. Both Lucas and Sarika stared into it as a dark shape rose slowly into view. It took several long moments for them both to register that this shape wasn't actually an animal—or human.

It was a monster in a suit of armor. As it lifted fully into sight, the helmet on top turned toward them, revealing its face to the pair. A cold stare showed no emotion whatsoever. The red eyes behind the mask didn't seem able to see either one of them properly. The monster stepped out of the elevator and walked right past them, moving like a machine. Lucas felt a chill go down his spine and reached out to find his hand brushing against Sarika's. He quickly pulled his hand back, confused by the sudden contact.

She looked at his hand and then back to him, her eyes even wider, if that was possible. "I've got a bad feeling about this," she whispered.

A dozen feet above, the monster paused and turned to face them with glowing red eyes. His hand came down, pointing.

"You are mine," he said. His voice sounded like thunder rolling through the tower. "I will be the one to deliver you to Simon."

He stomped, creating cracks in the floors

through which half a dozen creatures poured up from underground, each with a massive sword or ax in their hands. All aimed straight at Lucas and Sarika.

They were forced back against the wall of the elevator lobby, finding themselves pinned between the monsters and the doors. They couldn't move, and there seemed little chance of escaping without being cut down.

"I don't want to go with him," Lucas said in a panic.

Sarika nodded, her eyes wide. She looked over at the glass doors they had entered through. A brick wall slammed down to block the entrance as if in answer. The monsters stood there looking at them, their weapons raised.

Sarika took his hand and pulled. "We have to get to the elevator!"

She aimed her blaster at the nearest of the monsters, sending off blasts as they ran. The nearest creature howled as it pixelated out.

"XP in the real world," Sarika said with a chuckle and then turned to grin at Lucas. "Isn't that cool?"

"I'd rather not have monsters in our world, but... sure."

She laughed and prepared to fight. "Well, I guess

it depends on how leveling up in our world will affect us. And can everyone do it? Imagine getting into a fight at school and then gaining XP for it. Would bullies level up?"

"Ummm..."

"My guess is it'd be more like in those games where your appearance changes based on your actions. Now that *would* be awesome."

Before he could respond, the elevator doors opened and the other monsters turned their attention to the opening doors. Something, or somebody, was coming.

A woman who was maybe in her thirties stepped out through the doors. She wore a long white dress that flowed behind her as if in a soft breeze, and her hair was pure white, glistening in the light.

"Quick, come with me," the woman said and threw something out into the lobby. It hissed and then shot out smoke to give them cover.

"Go!" shouted Lucas.

Hand in hand, Sarika and Lucas ran toward the elevator and their new friend, knowing that whoever she was, she had to be better than these monsters.

They arrived at the elevator as the woman stepped forward, reaching into a pocket of her dress. She held up her hand so that a beam of energy shot out toward the monsters who had been waiting for their prey. The blast struck, and the closest of the monsters was instantly vaporized.

Lucas and Sarika slid into the elevator and then turned to see the monsters charging at them as the doors started to shut. Another blast from Sarika pixelated one out, and she made a giddy squeal.

"What?" Lucas asked in confusion, turning to her.

"Leveled up!"

Perfect timing, too, because the doors closed and, for the moment, the group was safe. She had her screen up, applying her skill points. Sarika noted that she was thinking of pursuing a shaman path because she wanted to be able to communicate with animals.

"That would be great," Lucas said but turned to the new woman and frowned, awkward silence taking over.

Sarika's breaths were heavy next to Lucas, and he realized his were as loud. Trying to find his calm, he turned to the woman with white hair and asked, "Who are you?"

"My name is Driana," she said, stepping forward and hitting the button for the top floor. "There's no time for introductions now. We need to get out of here."

A thud sounded. Scratching came a moment later. The monsters were trying to enter the elevator.

"We're ready," Sarika said, a blaster shaking in her hand.

Lucas took a deep breath, watching the numbers as the elevator ascended. He had dropped his sword at some point, he now realized, so he summoned it again.

"You're fighting Simon?" he asked Driana.

"I am."

"But I thought only kids were involved," Lucas admitted.

"What gave you that idea?"

More screeching and scratching distracted him, but he regained his focus. "Kids were missing and... I just assumed."

"Adults play games too." She hit the button to stop the elevator, starting to pry the doors apart. "We get out here—climb the rest. But yes, I'm fighting Simon. Have been since Ralli found me and clued me in. I was a game designer out of the Tokyo branch, and..."

Before she could continue her story, the doors opened to reveal a giant eye staring at them. It seemed to be part of the wall. It even blinked, and sure enough, the eyelids were metal!

Sarika stepped up and aimed her blaster at the wall before taking a shot. The screeching told them she had hit her mark. She fired again, then again, and was joined by Driana. Lucas let out a warrior call and threw his sword so it landed in the center of the large eye, causing it to vanish. This time it was his turn to gain XP but not level up yet.

With the eye gone, the passage ahead was clear.

"Run!" Driana said, and they all advanced. "This is bad. Simon must know where we are."

"But he doesn't know that Ralli came through to our world," Lucas replied. "She's our secret weapon."

6

MADISON

Madison held Ralli's gaze, pulling comfort from her confidence. With a deep breath and increased focus, she turned to the doors on Tokyo Tower that would lead to the spider monster. This was it, their chance to take the tower. There was no going back.

"Give it all you got," Ralli said, and they stepped out onto an upper observation deck.

Wind howled, bringing with it a chill. The view from Tokyo Tower almost made her forget the danger they were in.

From up here, she could see for miles in every direction. To the south, the sprawling metropolis of Tokyo was gray and glittering with its towering skyscrapers and bustling streets. To the north, he could see lush green forests and rolling hills. To the west were hints of water that she guessed was Tokyo Bay. On a clear day, she imagined she would even be able to see Mount Fuji in the distance but couldn't be sure with the heavy cloud cover that was moving in.

Soon, all the rest was covered in a haze, and a screeching reminded her that the spider was nearby.

"Maddi, pay attention!" Jacob shouted, running past her and swinging his ax. Perfect timing, too—a long, metal claw clanged against his ax, sending him stumbling back.

A split second later, the spider landed on the observation deck in front of them. It was twice as large as any man. Despite its spider body and eight legs, it had two arms with metal claws at the end of each. Red eyes glared at them, but it didn't attack again yet.

Instead, a digital image of Simon was projected from a device around its neck.

"There you are," Simon said, and he laughed. "Right where I want you."

"Maybe that's true, but maybe you're right where we want you!" Madison replied, not sure what to say but hoping for a good comeback here. Based on the way he laughed again, it hadn't been the best.

"You have no idea where I am!" he said. "And you

won't, because my spider friend here is going to see that you're drained and stored for when I decide I need you in the future. Maybe I'll turn you into a mindless zombie, doing my bidding. Or maybe I'll just throw you from the tower."

Madison gulped, her confidence momentarily fading. An arrow shot out from nearby, connecting with the device and making it explode! In an instant, the image of Simon that had been projected now vanished.

Madison turned to see that the shot had come from Easter, who grinned to show off her pointy dragon teeth and said, "Nobody threatens my friend."

"Thanks," Madison said and then drew her sword and focused her attention back on the spider. "What do you all say we squash this bug?"

"Too bad Lucas isn't here," Jacob said, taking a defensive stance next to her. "He so loves killing spiders."

Madison laughed and then held up her sword. "For Lucas!" As the others repeated the war cry, she charged forward. The creature rose up to reveal grey, web-like tentacles that crackled with purple electricity. It shot out more web, which Madison cut at with her sword. Jacob ran at her side, but a bit of webbing stuck below, and he tripped, a shock of electricity sending him into spasms before he hit the ground.

"Go, I got him!" Ralli said. She knelt next to the boy while providing cover fire with her blaster.

Arrows twanged from Easter, though the spider was quick to swipe them away with his claws. Fido barked and tried to get around back for a bite, but the spider was too fast, scurrying back and forth amid its attacks.

Ducking low, Madison avoided one of those claws. She came up swinging. Metal connected with metal to send a shock wave down her arms.

Time to rely on her powers instead. While each of her big moves took a third of her mana to use, she first went with her Shadow Move to escape the creature's reach with an explosion of darkness. Then, coming up a good ten paces or so away, she spun and thrust out her sword so it sent an explosive blast to connect with the creature's face.

Less than a third of her mana remained, or so her screen showed. Considering that mana was how her power reserves were measured, she had to be careful. It would replenish, but slowly. In situations like these, escape plans like the Shadow Move could be the difference between life and death.

The fact that all of this worked here on Earth was mind-boggling.

As she lunged back in for another attack, she was vaguely aware of Ralli sending ranged attacks from the right. Someone was shouting, but she was too focused on landing another blow to be aware of the rest.

Her next blow landed true. The spider creature hissed and screeched as it was struck, its metal exoskeleton ringing with the impact. It swung its tentacles wildly, trying to fend off the kids' attacks. But they were too fast, dodging and weaving as they struck again and again.

Ralli was hit by a bolt of purple lightning and went down with a grunt of pain. Jacob tried to help her, but he was grabbed by one of the spider's tentacles and swung through the air. A strike sent Easter over the edge, but she appeared with wings flapping a second later, just in time to catch Fido. Jacob was nearby, shouting and attacking, but the spider creature was too fast.

Madison was the only one left standing, and she knew she had to act fast. Gritting her teeth, she redoubled her efforts, striking at the spider with all her might. It blocked blow after blow until finally Madison decided she'd had enough.

Slamming her sword into the ground, she sent out shock waves that caused the monster to be stunned momentarily. That was all her friends needed, landing blast after blast and arrows galore. As the spider was starting to recover, Madison closed the distance and hefted up her sword with both hands, bringing it down with all she had.

Kaboom! The blast from her strike sent shockwaves through her enemy, blasting apart spiderwebs and freeing its captives. She stepped back, winded, and saw the spider stumble and even collapse.

Madison waited for her screen to pop up but nothing happened. Could it be that her metaverse connection was fading or something like that? She started to turn when movement caught her attention and the spider creature lashed out at her.

A metallic leg sliced too close for comfort, its sharp edge catching a clump of her hair to disconnect it from her head and send it flying. Madison ducked and summoned her sword to slice through one of the spider's legs, so it collapsed to the ground. Ralli was at her side with a stun attack that left the spider twitching.

"Attack it now, Maddison!" Easter shouted, arrows dinging off the spider's metal but at least causing a bit of a distraction.

Madison leaped up, sword above her head. She brought it down into a direct hit on the creature's head. Her sword sliced, and then it was over. The nearby kids watched in amazement as the spider disintegrated before their eyes, disappearing into a cloud of smoke.

Panting and out of breath, they looked at each other and grinned. They had done it.

"Talk about your tough exterminations," Ralli said, wiping sweat from her brow.

"You were amazing," Jacob said, grinning. "Better than Lucas could've done, I'm sure."

"You weren't so bad yourself."

Madison grinned as she watched her screen pop up and show that not only had that earned her 300 XP, but she had leveled up!

"We did it," Ralli said. "We took Tokyo Tower!"

Easter flew over to Madison's side and grinned. The creature's large eyes looked up at her in a cartoonish way, purple scales glistening.

"You really were something," Easter said. "I'm glad you're on my side."

"We're a team," Madison replied, "and an amazing one at that."

Their amazing team had control over Tokyo Tower! She turned, sword held up in the air victoriously as the wind blew through her black and pink hair. Up here on the top of Tokyo Tower, she looked out over the fog that covered the city and felt a hint of worry in spite of her victory.

"Don't fall!" Jacob called over.

She turned her attention to him, standing on the ledge below with Ralli and the two animal friends, Easter and Fido.

"Don't get distracted," Jacob continued. "The enemies aren't all gone!" He gestured below to the lower metal of Tokyo Tower and, sure enough, it was still swarming with monsters.

Madison sighed. This wasn't going how it was supposed to go. It never was when you're stuck fighting endless waves of monsters.

"We took the tower, but they're still coming," she said and then turned to Ralli. "Why?"

"One second," Ralli said, and she ran over to the middle of where the spider webs had been. Those monsters were coming up fast, but then Ralli turned and smiled widely with a blue, glowing crystal in her hand.

"Got it! The energy core."

As she said the words, a flash of blue light shot out. It was like a warm bath to Madison, but it caused the monsters on the tower to all vanish.

"Now it's official," Ralli said. "The tower is ours!"

Jacob and the pets let out a cheer, and Madison clapped her hands once followed by a thought as her screen was still open.

"Wait, I'm confused," she said, hand on her chin as she assessed the screen. "I get that XP was showing, but it just hit me... how are we leveling up in our world?"

Jacob shrugged, looking at his own screen as he had apparently leveled up as well. "Why not? It's pretty sweet."

"But this is the real world!"

"Madison, every world is a real world," Ralli pointed out. "You have to change how you're conceiving of your world and the others from now on. This is the metaverse we live in, where all worlds are not only traversable, but have overlap points and so much more. So yeah, you are leveling up because you brought that part of you from the other world, from my worlds. There are other worlds out there as well, so who knows what might be possible in the future. Make sense?"

"I guess," Madison said but shook her head. To a certain degree she understood what Ralli was saying but couldn't quite reconcile the fact that she was leveling up in her own world. To test it, she pulled up her skill chart and smiled to see that she had acquired two skill points. Now level nine, she quickly adjusted the screen to assign points to speed and strength. She could never have too many of either. That brought her speed to fifteen and her strength to thirteen. Next, to assign those skill points.

Her skill tree showed two available paths. One focused on her connection to Easter and, considering the upgrades so far, went a direction labeled "Dragon Rider." On the other path were skills related to her becoming a "Shadow Hunter." How could she possibly choose between two awesome paths?

She considered her skill tree and the path of Shadow Hunter that she had started down. She already had Shock Wave and Ranged Attack, and more recently that Shadow Move skill. Next, she could choose between Shadow Sight, which would allow her to sense enemies through walls, and Shadow Movement, which would allow her to travel via shadows. Both sounded awesome.

Then again, the Dragon Rider path looked pretty exciting. It offered her low-level skills, starting with an upgrade to Easter that would change her from simply resembling a dragon to being full dragon—

baby sized, but able to breathe fire. The other skill in that path was Saddle Summon, which wouldn't be useful until the dragon was larger, or Dragon Cloak, giving her the option to make Easter go invisible.

Skills on both paths looked promising, and the latter skills even more so.

For now, though, she had to think about which skill paths would be the most useful in the near future. If they needed to take towers like this, the most useful would probably be to continue the Shadow Hunter skills. With that in mind, she applied one skill point to Shadow Sight and the other to Shadow Movement. Later, she would most definitely pursue the Dragon Rider path as well because that just sounded too cool not to.

Now that she had leveled up, her mana was full again. She would be ready for whatever the enemy had to throw at them.

"You all gonna get that loot, or should I?" a voice said, coming from the doorway.

They all turned to see a Japanese teen grinning at them. Except, he wasn't only Japanese. He also had a green tint to his skin and large, pointy teeth jutting out from his bottom lip.

"Aki?" Madison asked.

Judging by the way Ralli repeated the name and

then ran over to hug the boy, this was him. When she pulled back, she looked him up and down and laughed. "Hot dang, it's good to see you again!"

"Excuse me, but... I thought you were a boy from our world," Jacob said. "Sooo what's up with the..." He gestured to his own teeth, grimacing awkwardly.

"Upgraded," Aki said.

Ralli beamed. "It looks super cool."

"Wait, so not only can we level up and add skill points and all that, but... we can adjust our avatars?"

"Only they aren't avatars anymore," Ralli pointed out. "More like real-world skins."

"Yeah, watch this." Aki waved a hand over his face, and he looked like a normal boy. Then he did it again, and the orc look was back. "I can only have one on at a time without access to an avatar creation portal, but I'm having a blast."

"Sick!" Jacob said with a laugh and was at his screen again, likely about to apply a new skin to himself.

"Skin?" Madison asked, still not sure she got the term.

"In games it's what they call the different looks you can have, basically," Aki explained.

"Such as..." Jacob dismissed his screen and turned to face them, his face now changed to look like a soldier with a skeleton special-ops mask and mohawk. "Ta-da!"

Madison got it and was half-tempted to go the unicorn route so that head-butting baddies would take on a whole new meaning, but in the moment she couldn't bring herself to waste any more time.

"We have to go get Lucas," she said. "He's going to love all of this. Is this tower clear?"

Ralli turned and did a quick scan of Tokyo Tower. "From what I'm reading, yes."

"Now that my friend is free, we can hold this tower with the other kids while you go and help your brother," Aki said.

He gestured to a boy and girl who were climbing out of spider webbing. "I mean, we'd love to help, but if you all are attacking Carrot Tower, that'll probably draw Simon's attention."

"Good thinking!" Madison said.

"Before you go, one thing." Aki leaned close, lowering his voice. "There are these two out there, a boy and girl—definitely siblings, maybe twins? They tried to infiltrate our group and pretended to be helping, but then betrayed us. I think they're working for Simon, and it's why we weren't able to take this tower before you arrived."

"You don't have their names?" Ralli asked.

"Sorry, not for both of them. But I heard someone refer to the boy as Kraken."

"Kraken?" Madison scoffed. "Thanks, we'll be on the lookout." She hated that now they not only had to look out for monsters but kids who were traitors to Earth.

Madison glanced over to see Ralli scanning the area where the spider had been slain and then looking at the nearby walls, even the sky around Tokyo Tower, mumbling to herself.

"Everything okay with you?" Madison asked.

"No! I was hoping it would be here, but..." Ralli lowered her hands and then shrugged. "Sorry, it's just that I was hoping to find the other energy cores here that Simon is using to bring the creatures from the metaverse in. Looks like he has them spread out, likely with one at Carrot Tower. Still, I was hoping I'd find more here and make it simple."

"Let's take Carrot Tower then and figure it out!" Madison offered but then noticed her stomach rumbling. "Also, all this talk about the tower is really making me crave—"

"Carrot cake?" Jacob exited from inside, one hand wiping frosting from his lips, the other carrying several small plastic packages. "One step ahead of you, and lucky us, they had a cake vending machine inside, just by the gift shop."

"Um, you had Japanese money on you?" Madison asked.

He nodded to one of Aki's buddies, who replied, "It was the least I could do, considering you saved our lives. Got it from the loot left behind when the monsters pixelated away."

"Speaking of loot..." Jacob grinned and then ran back to where the monsters had been defeated, scooping up whatever he could carry.

Madison quickly forgot her cravings when she saw that one of the packages contained red velvet cake with chocolate chunks—her favorite. She quickly scarfed down as much as she could while Ralli made plans with Aki for how to hold the tower and, more importantly, how to contact her in case they needed backup. Let them have the loot as long as she had that cake.

When they were done, Ralli turned to Madison and Jacob. Ralli arched an eyebrow at the way they were finishing off those cakes—with help from Fido and Easter.

"Give me a bite," she demanded. Jacob shared a lemon cake with her, and her face lit up at the taste of it. "Remind me to spend some time simply eating and enjoying Earth food when this is all over. But for now, Maddi, you ready?"

"Let's get to Carrot Tower!" Madison said, but then frantically glanced around.

"After a drink of water?" Jacob asked with a wink, tossing her a bottle of water. She downed half of it and slid the rest into an empty holster on her belt, ready for more action and to find her brother.

7

LUCAS

As Lucas and Sarika advanced up Carrot Tower with their new friend Driana in the lead, more monster screeches and snarls sounded from the floors below them. The building groaned as if alive.

"Wait," Sarika said as they approached a dark room, her hand on Lucas's arm. "Something's there in the darkness."

"Another monster," Lucas replied, sensing it too. But he knew they weren't going to reach the top without facing more monsters.

Maybe Sarika hadn't faced as many of them as he had, which would explain the grip she had on his arm that was starting to hurt.

Driana glanced back from the doorway that led to the darkness, motioning them on.

"We got this," Lucas whispered, taking Sarika's hand off his arm but then wrapping his arm in hers. "You good?"

She pulled him close and nodded. "In the other world it was one thing. But this... this is our world. I thought it was nothing big, but it's getting to me."

"Let's send them all back home. Together."

They stepped past Driana, entering the darkened room first. The glow of Lucas's sword lit up a glimpse of something moving to the left. Lucas spun, trying to see what it was, but something smacked him in the face.

More movement. The blue glow from the sword stopped on a creature that resembled a turkey, proud and ready to strike again! The demon turkey's feathers were a mottled gold and green, iridescent in the low light. It had talons that were as sharp and curved as serrated blades. The demon turkey's screeches were an unholy combination of nails on a chalkboard, a banshee's scream, and the sound of steel being ground. A whiff of decay and rot hit Lucas's nose before the demon turkey struck again, hitting Lucas with a slap of its wing!

Lucas wasn't about to let this stupid bird slap him like that and get away with it. His sword forming in his hand, he charged. The demon turkey hissed, screeching its own attack. Lucas slashed, swiped, and lunged, trying to fend off the demonic bird. But the turkey was fast, its movements agile and sharp. It darted in and out of his reach, swooping down to peck or claw at him with its sharp talons. Lucas managed to land a couple of blows, but they only seemed to agitate the demon turkey further. It screeched and flapped its wings wildly, trying to fly away. But Lucas was right on its tail, slicing madly at it with his sword.

Nearby, Sarika was fighting off two more of these turkey demons with the help of their new friend. When Lucas thought he was about to win, the demon turkey struck again. It lunged at him from the side, sinking its claws deep into his shoulder and knocking him back onto the ground. The talons dug into his skin, piercing deeper as the demon turkey continued to slash and peck at him relentlessly.

Using all of his strength, he landed the final blow against his turkey. To his relief, it pixelated out like the other summoned monsters. More XP! That was always a welcome sight.

"Well done," Driana said, both of the others having finished off their opponents and watching as he did the same.

He gave them a brief nod, wanting nothing more

than to move on and forget all about this weird fight. Thanksgiving would never feel the same again, and he was pretty sure he would ask for ham if given the choice.

Driana led them away from the elevator and through a series of corridors that seemed to twist and turn in every direction. Finally, she stopped and pointed to a doorway with a small window set into the center of it.

"Here we are," said Driana, placing a hand on Lucas's shoulder. "Enter quickly."

"Why?" asked Lucas.

"Because there might be more of them," she said.

"Enough," Sarika cut in. "You have to tell us who you really are and what you are doing here right now!"

"I..." She turned to Lucas, bit her lip, and then continued. "I worked for your father before he went missing. In some ways, I'd like to think I still do."

Lucas stared in shock, completely forgetting about the drumming and sound of monsters throughout the building.

"You knew my dad?"

"It's a long story, one I can't get into now. Suffice it to say, I think he's still out there. Considering everything that's going on... I think we can get him back."

Lucas's heart skipped a beat and he staggered, glad to have Sarika there to help him stand.

She leaned in close and asked, "Sorry, your dad..."

"Gone. Some thought maybe... passed on." He shook his head, realizing they didn't have time for him to go weak or lose himself to thought and the questions that flew through his head. But he had to ask.

Catching up with Driana, Lucas asked, "You're sure he's alive?"

"Last time I saw him he was still breathing, yeah. I thought he was losing it, especially when he told me he was going in to try and stop Simon. But then all of this, so... Maybe he failed, maybe he succeeded. I don't know."

"You're talking about his father!" Sarika said. "Can't you have some compassion!"

Driana glanced back, frowned, and then shrugged. "At this point, we're all fighting for survival. Sugarcoating the truth won't do any of us any good."

Sarika's eyes narrowed, and she stepped toward

the woman, but Lucas noticed a shadow move ahead.

He raised a hand and said, "No, she's right. I don't want to get my hopes up, but if there's a chance my dad's out there, and if he really knew about all of this... I'll do everything I can to find and rescue him. Regardless, right now we need to focus."

Indicating the shadow movement ahead, he gestured toward a side hall with the sign for exit above, and they nodded. The three snuck off in that direction.

Lucas watched as Driana crept down the dimly lit hallway, her heart pounding. He and Sarika followed close behind, both of them looking up at her with wide, scared eyes. They could hear the shadow monster prowling just around the corner, its ragged breathing and the sound of its claws scraping against the floor sending shivers down their spines.

Driana signaled for them to stay close as she edged closer to the corner, trying to get a glimpse of the monster. As she peered around the edge, the shadow monster came into view, standing just a few feet away with its form flickering and shifting as it reached out with long, spindly fingers. Driana quickly pulled back, her heart racing.

She turned to Lucas and Sarika and put a finger

to her lips, silently signaling for them to be quiet. She gestured for them to follow her as she started to edge along the wall, trying to stay as far away from the monster as possible.

Lucas and Sarika followed her lead, moving as quietly as they could as they snuck past the shadow monster. Lucas held his breath, praying they wouldn't be noticed. His mind was still spinning with questions about his dad, but the danger at hand distracted him.

Finally, they reached the end of the hallway and slipped through the door, relieved to have made it past the shadow monster. They collapsed against the wall, panting and shaking with fear.

Driana turned to Lucas and Sarika, her eyes filling with tears of relief. "We made it," she whispered, hugging them tightly. "We're safe now."

It hit Lucas then that this woman, even if she was an adult, was no warrior. She was here trying to survive – to do her part but nothing more.

"Let's keep going," Lucas said.

Driana held his gaze, seemingly finding confidence. She gave him a nod before turning to keep moving. They rushed through the corridors as quietly as possible, trying to avoid the strange creatures lurking in the halls. Lucas wasn't sure if these were monsters from the metaverse or perhaps local people who had been zombified or affected by evil magic. He had no idea what Simon was capable of at this point.

Lucas knew they needed to find the entry points Simon was using to bring in the monsters. If Carrot Tower was being used for this purpose, they had to find it. As they reached a particularly dark and intimidating hallway, and their new friend went on to have a look ahead, Lucas turned to Sarika and asked, "Are you sure we can do this?"

Sarika's eyes were filled with fear, but she squeezed his hand firmly. "We don't have a choice. Do we?" She even managed to smile.

"Is something funny?" Lucas asked, confused.

"Only that I can feel your heartbeat through your hand. And I thought mine was going fast," Sarika replied.

As Lucas thought about it, he realized he could feel her heartbeat too. He placed his other hand on hers, focusing on the steady rhythm and finding it soothing. He looked ahead at the flickering shadows and the darkness that seemed to swirl like inverted light. He knew a monster was waiting for them.

With a deep breath, he let go of Sarika's hands and stood up. "We got this," he said, trying to convince himself as much as her. In his mind, he hoped his sister and Ralli were on their way to find them and would be able to help them in this situation. Hopefully, the two were keeping Jacob out of trouble.

Lucas waited until the last moment to conjure his sword, as its light could draw attention. He signaled for Sarika to stay back and peeked out to see what lay ahead.

As he suspected, a creature was pacing in front of them, but their companion was nowhere to be found. That's when the creature turned to look at them, revealing that it was their new friend, Driana. Only now her eyes glowed red and claws made of shadow extended from her hands. How had this occurred?

She hadn't seemed malevolent, so he couldn't believe that she had just transformed. Could it be another version of her? Or... no! He saw it now, a shadow creature on the ceiling, manipulating its hands with what seemed to be shadow strings hanging down. Somehow this creature was controlling her, like a shadow puppeteer.

8

MADISON

Madison and her group darted through the streets of Tokyo, following a map from Ralli's holographic projection that showed the way to Sangenjaya, where Carrot Tower and her brother awaited. The farther they went, the more clouds lowered to surround them. A strange fog rolled in and growls of monsters sounded.

Ralli paused to check the map. "We better end this soon before more people are taken by Simon."

Madison nodded, leading the charge.

The girls and Jacob with their pets ran in a pack through buildings and over streets. Buildings shook and screeched. Madison and Ralli threw themselves into the cover of a tall building's entrance just before a large monster appeared in front of them. Two other monsters crouched on either side of it as it snarled and roared at them. Madison charged it with Ralli on her heels.

The monster bellowed and leaped over its companions toward Madison as she charged head-long. Its mouth opened wide as it tore across the ground toward her with a roar that could have shattered glass. She kept running and ducked below the monster, slamming it into the wall as she jumped back to her feet.

Jacob appeared at her side and slammed his ax into the monster so a fireball burst out of the monster as it hit the wall and exploded into glass shards and chunks of rubble. Madison ducked as shrapnel rained down on her and Ralli, but none struck their skin. They looked up at the monster as its body pixelated out of existence in front of them.

Madison felt like her energy was drained, so she paused, checking her stats. She looked at Ralli as she shivered and rubbed her arms where she had smacked into the wall. Her floating display appeared, showing an increase in XP.

"I still think it's soooo cool that we can level up even here. Not that it makes any sense."

"Strange, but I suppose it makes sense, considering that the worlds are now more linked," Ralli replied. She held up her arms to show two bracelets she hadn't had before. "I've been doing it, and look —these produce energy shields. Should come in handy!"

"I bet!"

As a demonstration, Ralli made an X with her arms. A circle of energy shot out in front of her to form a protective barrier the size of a kitchen table.

The prospect of leveling up and upgrades on Earth would have made Madison more excited if she'd had her brother there to celebrate with her. They couldn't waste any more time getting to Carrot Tower to save him. They would have to make do with each other for now. She turned her attention back to their surroundings as they ran through Tokyo, dodging monsters in every direction.

As they ran, Madison used Shadow Sight to see silhouettes of monsters behind walls. Using this skill, they were able to avoid most monsters. However, as they passed a metro station, a rumbling sounded, and the ground exploded up in their path. Through it came a monster as large as a house. Its skin was cracked like beaten leather and its hair was patchy, simmered in places, and burned off in others. Madison launched herself out of the way with a jump over its head just as it slammed full force into the wall behind them. Ralli possessed no such speed and hit it just as hard before falling to the ground with a thud that shook all three of them.

The monster turned toward them and roared, but Madison kept her eyes on it as she started a mental countdown in her head, assessing how much time they had before it made any move toward them. Three seconds later, it charged again. She turned toward Ralli and motioned for her to follow as she jumped from her crouching position to leap at the monster while it was distracted by Madison's antics.

Madison burst into the air with a Shadow Move and then landed on its back with a kick that sent them both flying and crashing onto a nearby building corner. It snarled at them angrily and stood up, colliding with Madison head-on with its arms open like wings.

"Watch out!" Jacob shouted. He tried to work his way over to her, only for the monster's tail to lash out and send him tumbling across the ground.

Madison jumped off its back and landed on one side of Jacob while Ralli landed on its other side as they regained their footing.

"You two okay?" Madison asked.

Jacob nodded, his face fixed on the monster in

front of him with his ax outstretched to ward off any attack from their opponent.

Madison looked at their monster and felt a sense of calm spread through her as if she were meditating as they sometimes did in her school's PE class. She had always wondered how meditating had anything to do with PE, but now she got it. The best way to fight was with a clear mind. Her calm came from a place of normalcy. After all their adventures on the other side of the metaverse, this was familiar territory for her, and she knew how to fight monsters like this one.

Jacob nodded slowly. He looked over at Ralli where she stood quietly behind Madison with her war hammer poised for action against their opponent. She nodded at him in return before launching into motion against their monster. Jacob lunged as well and swung with his ax only to miss! He almost lost the weapon but recovered in time to turn and block a strike from the monster.

Madison leaped into action, determined to destroy this monster.

"On me!" she shouted, jumping up to give herself some height against their opponent while Ralli ran to catch up with her.

Except, as they fought, Madison noticed another

monster nearby—above, watching them. The creature had a demonic face of blue with gold horns and blond hair streaming out from its head, a body of flowing colors and no shape as if it were one with the wind.

"Another monster!" she shouted, pointing.

For some reason, it was watching and not attacking. Madison and her friends focused their attack on the monster above. She leaped and flew over the monster's head with more of her Shadow Move skill. Madison landed to slam into its backside with both feet before diving onto its back for leverage.

From there, she landed a hit hard enough to knock it forward into Ralli's waiting arms. Ralli caught the monster with her war hammer, and then Madison hit it with her massive sword. It pixelated out of existence as she landed back on her feet.

"Great work!" Ralli said, beaming at Madison. "We're getting better at this! Let's keep going!"

Madison watched her XP rising enough to be close to leveling up again and then turned to face Jacob, who pushed himself up and gave them an appreciative nod.

But the other creature was still above, its flowing colors shooting out around her. One look at it with its Kimono and the two horns growing up from its forehead made her think it had to be an "Oni," or a Japanese demon of sorts. She only knew that because her brother talked about all his nerd obsessions so often.

The Oni thrust its hands out to both sides, wind howling as it picked up and threatened to knock Madison off her feet.

"Not bad," the Oni said in a girl's voice, shouting above the howling wind. "But how is it you Earthlings have grown so much in strength?"

A gust of wind hit, but then the air went still. The Oni descended upon them. The creature flew at Madison, its eyes only inches from her face. The icy blue orbs stared out from behind what was clearly a mask! Was she a monster or a human?

Either way, the attack came next and Madison was forced to defend herself. Already low on mana, she had to rely on her own speed and strength. She lifted her sword to block a strike of long claws before trying to go on the attack, only to feel the wind knock her off her feet. Madison hit the ground hard and rolled, coming up with another block.

"I got you!" Easter shouted, flying in for the attack. Wind hit and Easter's wings didn't do much good. As hard as she flapped, all the small dragon could do was spiral in circles to avoid slamming into a lamp post.

Jacob and Fido tried to help too, but it wasn't until Ralli leaped into the fray that they began to make any headway. A flash of light transformed Ralli into a bear with long claws, like her friend Christy—who had been a creation of hers!—had been that first time Madison and the others had met her. That at least helped her stand her ground against the wind, but the Oni was too fast, circling around and slashing with its claws.

Ralli sent out sparks from her bear claws while Jacob slashed with his ax, but none of them were able to hit the Oni. At least, not until Madison saw that she had enough mana again to strike. She managed to get out a blast from her sword that flew into the air, unwavering from the wind, and hit.

The Oni momentarily lost control of the wind but turned to face her with a laugh. "So, you aren't completely helpless after all!"

"Come down here and fight us!" Madison said. "Stop flitting about up there!"

"I'll give you that you're very powerful," the Oni said, riding the wind up again but cocking her head and listening to the shouting. "But I don't have time to deal with y'all right now. So sorry, but I'll have to let the fog finish you off."

She was up and riding the wind in a flash, gone from there.

"What was that?" Jacob asked, a hand to his chest. "A real Oni? Right? Japanese demon or protector or something?"

"I don't know about that," Ralli replied. "What I do know is that she wasn't entirely from another world—more like a hybrid. Someone from here mixed with a monster, perhaps?"

"Let's hope we don't run into her again," Easter said, curling up next to Madison, circling her leg and grabbing onto her side.

Madison agreed the Oni had been troublesome but would have preferred to fight it right then instead of worrying about the creature showing up later. Her unease turned to curious worry as the fog rolled in. A distant screaming caused Madison to shiver.

"What's up with the fog?" Jacob said, his voice quivering.

Madison gave it some thought. "My bet... Simon's making it happen. To confuse us."

"Maybe even unwittingly," Ralli added, preparing to fight at her side. "Might be a sign of converting Earth to become part of the true metaverse."

"Wait, what?"

"A true inter-dimensional existence where all worlds cross over. Virtual and otherwise, we all share the ability to move through these different states of existence. Not just a multiverse, but a meta-verse. *The* metaverse, greater than any of your Earth futurists could have predicted."

"Whoa..." Jacob looked like he'd just had his mind opened for the first time.

"Let's keep moving," Madison said, indicating a path ahead between two tall buildings.

All three of them and the two pets turned left down an alleyway between two buildings that led straight to Carrot Tower when something else came to life nearby with a screech that sounded like nails on chalkboard followed by roars that echoed through.

Not only that, the fog nearly blocked their path, closing in quickly.

"Run!" Madison shouted and sprinted with all she had.

The screams grew louder, along with the cries of monsters howling into their ears from all sides as they reached Carrot Tower. Finally, they'd made it.

9

LUCAS

Driana continued to pace the floor in Lucas's path, her eyes red and strange lines of shadow flowing up from her to the Shadow Puppeteer above. Lucas and Sarika couldn't figure a route past her no matter which direction they turned. Worse, they didn't want to leave Diana behind—not like this.

"Have you dealt with whatever that is?" Lucas whispered to Sarika.

She shook her head, stretching her exoskeleton legs. "I never even had puppets growing up."

"I-I don't think that would have helped us much here anyway."

"Just saying."

"We're going to be okay," he said, as much to reassure himself as her.

"I know. Doesn't make me any less scared."

He frowned, wondering what she meant by knowing they would be okay. Considering that they had faced many dangerous enemies, they certainly could be okay—but their safety was certainly not guaranteed!

An urge came over him to take her hand and hope some of her confidence would come his way. Instead, he simply nodded and muttered, "We got this."

Lucas had a thought. Their abilities worked in the real world, but he hadn't yet tried to use all of his skills. Since he had been following a Beast Master skill path, he had one or two tricks up his sleeve.

"I'm going to distract it," he said, his knees bent and prepared to run. "That is, if this works."

Sarika gave him an excited glance. She had seen what he was capable of back in the misfit world. "Do your thing."

"Come on, wolves," Lucas said, his voice barely a whisper.

A second later, he had summoned his three blue, semi-translucent wolves. At his mental command, they charged forward. They kept to the right wall so that when they redirected their movement toward the Shadow Puppeteer, she would think the attack was coming from a different direction.

Meanwhile, Lucas motioned for Sarika to follow him to the left. Since the Shadow Puppeteer had Driana under its control, they couldn't simply avoid it.

Speaking of her, Driana had just turned her red eyes to the wolves, meaning her back to Lucas. Above, the Shadow Puppeteer was no longer visible.

"Move," Lucas hissed, about to take the lead. Except, before he had even taken one step, Sarika darted out ahead of him, heading for an exit to the left. He followed close behind, but a growl from his wolves told him there was trouble.

He reached the hallway and turned, surprised to see no sign of Driana or the wolves!

"Sarika," he whispered, ducking around the corner and then slowly leaning back again to take a look.

"Boo!" Driana's red eyes were an inch away from him.

He nearly attacked, but had to restrain himself since he didn't want to hurt the woman being used by the Shadow Puppeteer. Instead, he stumbled back and only summoned his sword for a block as a shadow moved his way from overhead.

"Thanks," Sarika said, appearing behind Driana. Where had she come from?

As she moved, she jumped and her flying snowboard appeared under her feet. Lucas wasn't sure of her plan, but he knew he needed to do his part. Kicking off of the nearby wall, he flew away from Driana and struck at the ground with his sword to create a loud clang and a spark.

It worked! Above Driana, the Shadow Puppeteer's shadow strings appeared and then the creature came into sight, focused on him. Meanwhile, Sarika fell back and kicked, sending her snowboard to go flying. The snowboard hit the shadow strings and cut right through!

Driana stumbled toward Lucas, the red clearing from her eyes.

"We need to run," she said, grabbing Lucas by the shoulder before turning with a gasp. Lucas saw and heard why. The Shadow Puppeteer had pulled up with a screech, turning its attention toward Sarika.

Sarika recovered to stand her ground as the Shadow Puppeteer advanced on her, its shadow strings writhing and snapping in the air.

She drew her gleaming knife. "Come on then,"

she shouted, brandishing the weapon. "I'm not afraid of you."

The Shadow Puppeteer hesitated as if surprised by Sarika's boldness. But then it lunged forward, its shadow strings darting toward her like venomous snakes.

Sarika was ready, though. She dodged and weaved, her knife flashing as she cut through the shadow strings one by one. The Shadow Puppeteer hissed and screeched, its movements becoming more frenzied as it struggled to catch Sarika. But then it lunged forward, its shadow strings darting toward them like venomous snakes. One almost hit her, but Lucas lunged in at the right moment, his lava sword deflecting the shadow.

He took his place next to her. Driana put a hand to her mouth, and Lucas knew he needed to keep the attention away from her.

"Come and get us, monster!" he shouted.

The monster lunged, but he had a trick up his sleeve. The wolves had vanished before, but he brought them back now for the attack. They lunged and distracted the monster. Although it spun and caught them so that they disappeared, that was all Sarika and Lucas needed. Both lunged to attack at once.

Lucas tried to keep up with Sarika as she dodged and weaved, her knife flashing as again she cut through the shadow strings one by one. He swung wildly with his sword, trying to connect with the creature while being careful not to hurt Sarika in this closed space.

"Watch out!" Driana shouted.

Lucas turned just in time to see a shadow string hurtling toward him. He ducked and rolled, narrowly avoiding being trapped.

Sarika redoubled her efforts, her blade a blur as she struck repeatedly. The Shadow Puppeteer howled in pain and rage, its movements becoming more frenzied as it struggled to catch her.

But Sarika was too quick and skilled. She danced around the Shadow Puppeteer, her blade a blur as she attacked. The creature howled in pain and rage, its shadow strings disintegrating under Sarika's relentless assault.

Finally, with a cry of defeat, the Shadow Puppeteer disintegrated into a cloud of swirling darkness, leaving Sarika and Lucas standing victorious amidst the wreckage.

Screens popped up and XP came flooding in from their victory, bringing Lucas's level to seven. He looked at the stats briefly, seeing he had two new skill points, and grinned. He quickly looked at his skill tree to see he could get an ability that let him ride the wolves, so he took it. The second skill point could wait because at the moment, Sarika was doing a fun little dance that he had to watch. Not all that graceful, but cute in its own way.

"That's how it's done," Sarika said, turning to Driana with a triumphant grin and finishing up her victory dance. "No one messes with us and gets away with it."

She was proud, but Lucas was too busy being annoyed to celebrate quite yet. Turning to her with chest heaving, he let his sword vanish and said, "You used me as bait!"

"I had no choice," she replied. "Worked, didn't it?"

"And almost got you killed!"

"Enough," Driana interrupted. "It's over now, and the two of you saved me. We need to get to the top and finish this."

Lucas and Sarika shared a look that said they agreed, but that didn't mean he wasn't annoyed. He was about to say they should hurry and move on when he noticed movement from the corner of his eye. Spinning, he came face to face with a boy whose expression was intense like he had just swallowed the spiciest of peppers.

"Kraken?" Sarika asked.

"You're with them now?" the boy asked as he took a step forward. Oddly, the boy flickered like a light about to go out.

"I am, and you can join us too," Sarika replied. "It's not too late."

The boy shook his head. "Nah. You don't know what Simon's capable of. I'd watch out if I were you. Simon has it out for those friends of yours, and if you're with them that puts you in his sights. Give that some thought, and when you're ready to join me... say the word."

With a final glare in Lucas's direction, the boy known as Kraken flickered again and then vanished.

Lucas eyed Sarika, wondering if she was at all tempted by this boy's offer. Not wanting to dwell on it, he pointed and said, "To the top!"

Leading the way, he bounded up the stairs and burst through the door to find they had made it.

He stood in place taking in the large room surrounded with windows for viewing of the surrounding Tokyo area. Surprisingly, he saw no sign of Simon. All the room contained was a floating crystal—a blue, shimmering gemstone that glowed with an inner light. It hovered in the air, suspended by some unseen force, and pulsed with a strange, otherworldly energy.

Lucas had played enough games to understand that this was likely the item Simon was using to summon the creatures from another world. Somehow, he had found a way separate from Ralli's key that he had been after.

As he looked upon the crystal, Lucas couldn't help but feel a sense of awe and dread. He knew he couldn't let it fall into the wrong hands. He had to find a way to destroy it, or at least keep it hidden and out of reach.

"The Shadow Puppeteer was the dungeon's boss," Lucas said, stepping up to the crystal and eyeing it with awe.

"Apparently," Sarika replied.

"This isn't a dungeon. It's the real world," Driana said. "But... yeah. Pretty much."

"Why isn't Simon here?" Lucas asked.

"Most likely, this isn't the only one," Driana replied. "By my understanding, he wouldn't be able to summon the creatures of the metaverse without several crystals. Not in the state he was in. And while the crystals are in effect, he could create other colors, like on a color wheel—blue and yellow make green. You get the picture."

"And we have to take them all?" Sarika asked.

"Possibly... There might be another way, but for now..." She suddenly turned to them, her eyes narrowed on Lucas. "Do you have anything of your mom's?"

"What? Why?"

"If this acts like the key, which I believe it does, we should be able to each use it as a teleport point once. You need to reconnect with your sister, but... I can go after your mom, get her to safety."

"I don't... I mean, you think my mom's in danger?"

Driana nodded. "But we're not too late. Simon will be pursuing her because I think she'll be the key to getting your dad back."

Lucas gulped, not quite sure he had heard those words correctly. "I'm still trying to process the idea that my dad might be out there, somewhere... waiting for us to find him."

"When I worked for your dad, he had so much going on, so many secrets. Your dad didn't just disappear, Lucas. He went into the metaverse, taken to another world, as a sacrifice to save us all. I didn't believe it at the time, and neither did your mom. We both thought he was crazy, but now it's clear he wasn't."

Lucas's eyes narrowed in determination. "I'll go to the ends of the Earth if needed... and beyond!" His hands moved over his pockets, but he couldn't think of what they might use. His left hand moved across the button. When his pants had broken a few months back, his mom had taken a button from one of her jackets and sewn it on. "This was hers," he said and snapped it off.

"It should do." Driana took the button, eyeing the crystal. "If we can use these crystals to locate him, we might be able to get him back. He worked with Simon and might be the secret to stopping all of this."

There was a chance to bring his Dad back, to put an end to Simon's twisted plans. That thought alone was enough to push Lucas forward.

"We have to do everything we can to bring my dad home."

"I'll get your mom to safety. You... you find your sister and make contact with me at this number." She took out a business card and handed it over.

"People still use these?" Lucas asked, eyeing the phone number and email address on it.

"Some adults do."

Holding that button, she approached the crystal.

"Wait!" Lucas said, his hand outstretched toward her. "How-how do we know you're really with us? Not an agent for Simon?"

"Smart question," she replied. "You have my card, so you can use one of these portals to jump to me at any time. Other than that, all I can say is that I'm on your side, and I hope you believe me."

Lucas looked at Sarika, who nodded.

"Okay," he said.

Blue light flashed from the crystal as Driana stepped toward it. The light expanded outward, showing a building that Lucas recognized as his mother's office. In a flash, the light took Driana! It vanished and she was gone, leaving that glowing crystal and no sign of her.

"Wow," Sarika said, transforming her exoskeleton legs back into her wheelchair. As she sat, she let out a sigh of relief and awe.

"Double wow," Lucas agreed and then started circling the crystal and wondering how he was going to get to his sister. A glance out through the windows showed a flash of blue light that shot out from the building, and the fog pulled back.

By taking the crystal, it seemed, they had cleared Carrot Tower. He wouldn't have been surprised to find out that any remaining creatures were no longer under the control of Simon.

10

MADISON

Madison and team had been fighting their way up the stairs and were now face to face with an orange monster with horns and sharp teeth. Its red eyes glared at them, claws at the ready. Madison was exhausted, quite ready to be done with this.

Still, she would do what was necessary. Taking a step forward and preparing to summon her massive sword again, she heard a sound like a bell chiming. Immediately following the sound, a blue blast of light flew down and past them.

When it had passed, the monster knelt and then slowly turned to face them. It seemed to... smile? Madison hesitated, not sure what to do.

"Ralli?" it asked, red eyes turning green, glow fading.

"Wait, is that you, Xalda?" Ralli leaped forward and hugged the creature that, only seconds ago, Madison had been sure was going to try and kill them.

Ralli beamed, turning back to her. "It would seem your brother took Carrot Tower. It's ours!"

"Use the key to give him a call," Ralli said. "It should work. My guess is the towers were causing some sort of signal distortion, intercepting even. So... go on."

Madison blinked in confusion, watching as Ralli's new friend gave them a wave and headed down the stairs, saying it was going to check on its friends. Holding up the key, Madison focused on her brother and said, "Lucas? Can you hear me?"

Waiting for a response, she started to imagine a final fight that could have resulted in her brother getting injured. Was he up there somewhere, lying unconscious or worse... at death's door?

"I'm here," Lucas finally said, and then his face appeared in the hologram that the key projected.

"You did it," Ralli said. "Congrats."

"I'm so proud of you," Madison added, thinking she could see her brother blushing. "Enough of this gushiness. We still have a lot of stairs, but we're on our way to you."

"Wait, you might not need to," Lucas said. And a moment later, a portal appeared on the stairs between Madison and her friends. "I was able to form a connection thanks to this crystal. Come on!"

"On our way," Madison replied, motioning the others to join her as she stepped into the portal.

A second later, she was on the top floor of Carrot Tower, grinning at her brother.

"Finally!" Lucas said with a smile. He looked up at a window with a diamond pattern embedded in its glass. "Did you find Simon?"

She shook her head. "Not yet. No sign of him here?"

"None," Sarika said.

"But we met a woman who used to work with Dad," Lucas added. "Said she thinks he's out there, and we can find him thanks to the portals."

Madison gulped, unable to believe this. Her head swiveled. "Where is she now?"

"Went to find Mom to get her to safety."

"Oh, no..." Madison hadn't even thought about how all this could be used to hurt the people they loved. She turned to Jacob with concern. "And what about your parents?"

"Or mine," Sarika said, rolling her wheelchair up next to them.

Ralli cleared her throat. "I wouldn't worry about either of your families," she said to Jacob and Sarika. "Ever since we connected to the systems back there, I've been monitoring to check for info while also putting up any protections I can."

"And our mom?" Madison asked.

"Of course—but this woman probably has the right idea. My protections only go so far. You said she worked with your father?"

"Yeah. Called herself Driana."

"She's with me, but I didn't make the connection earlier." Ralli put a hand to her chin, thinking, and then nodded. "Your father... I didn't process that it was him before, but now I'm starting to think I might have had some interaction with him early on. He never named himself, but... It's all coming together."

"Really?" Madison asked.

"We'll have to confirm it all when we find him, but yes. A man was working with Simon, only at one point he vanished."

"According to Driana, he sacrificed himself to protect our world," Sarika chimed in.

"Oh, you must be Sarika," Jacob said, thrusting out a hand. "Good to meet you in person. I mean, not as Stryka."

"Same," she replied, but ignored his hand and

gave him a quick hug. Next, she did the same for Madison and then Ralli.

"Glad to have you here with us," Ralli said. "I wish the same could be said for all the others, but Simon's offer was too tempting."

Madison frowned, nodding. She wished her new friend Adle could have been there with them as well but figured it was best to keep as many out of danger as possible. Maybe the girl didn't want to get involved again, anyway, so it was best to let her be.

"Okay, so about this woman?" Sarika asked.

"And what's this about her going to Mom?" Madison chimed in, heart thudding at the idea that her dad might be out there somewhere, and that they could possibly see him alive again.

"We have her contact," Lucas said, holding up a card.

"But not yet," Ralli said.

Madison turned to her. "What?"

"I know it's not what you want to hear, but we're not ready. If you want to bring your father back, we need to clear the final prime gateway. There should be three of them, and we've cleared two."

Everyone turned to her, waiting for more of an explanation.

"It's about triangulating the signal," Ralli said.

Madison frowned, wondering if she understood what sort of advanced scientific or magical procedure Simon was using.

"So let me get this straight," Madison said. "You're saying we need to use three points of reference to determine the location of a portal, and then use that information to create the portal and bring monsters over from another world?"

Ralli nodded. "Right. Triangulating the signals means using the magic of these crystals to detect and measure the energy signatures of the three reference points and then using that data to calculate the coordinates of the portal."

"But we've disrupted it, right? Made it so they won't work anymore?"

"Maybe, for now. With the other crystals I'm sure he's managed to make by now... it's only a matter of time."

Lucas stepped forward, looking quite brave. Madison certainly liked this new side of him instead of the nerdy gamer she had known him to be for most of his life.

"So we go out there and find it," he said.

"And use them to send the monsters back," Ralli added enthusiastically.

"But how do we find it?" Jacob asked.

"The fog, for one," Madison said. "And anywhere there's an attack, right?"

"That should work, but we need to find the third prime to be able to do so. The other crystals won't do the trick."

"What are we waiting for?" Lucas asked.

"I don't think it'll be so easy," Ralli countered. "Simon will find out that we've taken two of his towers, if he doesn't already know. Let's get a bite to eat, observe, and be sure to make our next move on a full stomach."

"Really? At a time like this, you want to eat?!" Madison gestured to the crystal. "We have to stop him, we have to..." She stopped, realizing Ralli was probably right. With all the fighting and running around, she was exhausted and practically starving.

Everyone agreed it was time to eat, so they headed down to the first floor of Carrot Tower. On the way, they passed more than one monster they had defeated earlier. Only now, the monsters were milling about and doing their own thing. They weren't trying to attack them anymore. The red from their eyes was gone, and it seemed they were curious about this world. They looked like a bunch of puppies unleashed to have a good time.

Indeed, a group of monsters that looked very

much like puppies were standing on their hind legs and working their way into a vending machine full of sandwiches.

"Are you seeing this?" Lucas asked.

"I'm kind of liking it," Madison replied. She looked at him, still feeling the tingles of joy that came with having been reunited with her brother and finding him still alive. She felt a mix of relief and happiness, having thought he might have been dead.

One of the monsters looked their way and grinned, and one even spoke.

"Wow, this place is amazing!" the monster said. Its voice was like that of a young child. "But I'm kind of scared. Do you know how to get back home?"

Madison wanted to run to the little creature and give it a hug, to tell it that everything was going to be okay. Instead, she just looked to Ralli for an answer.

"We're working on it," Ralli said.

The craziest part wasn't even that these monsters were in the tower, but that when the kids all exited, they saw more monsters starting to spread out into town. People in the businesses and homes were scared at first but then showed curiosity. A young boy approached one of the monsters that looked like something straight out of a children's movie and even started to scratch its head behind the ears.

Madison held up a hand, about to shout for the kid to stop before it got attacked, but Ralli shook her head and said, "Wait."

She was right. The monster didn't attack but instead rolled over to show the kid its belly. Soon the child began to tickle the monster's belly, and the monster was giggling.

"It's just so weird," Jacob said, but then he ran forward and started tickling the monster as well.

Madison and Lucas shared a look of surprise and then both laughed.

Sarika shook her head with confusion and turned to Ralli. "Is this going to be our new norm?"

"I don't think so, but if we can't stop Simon... who knows." Ralli gestured around to several other monsters. One was large like King Kong, climbing the side of the building. It had bright yellow fur and long flowing green hair like silk out of its back. "I know Japanese people are better prepared than any for this, based on their movies and manga, but still. We have to fix this."

A scream sounded from nearby, and they all turned to see a businesswoman outside of a convenience store with a broom in her hand, trying to fend off some little critters. These ones looked more like goblins but with skin that was dark purple. They didn't seem to be trying to hurt her, but Madison knew as well as any of them that they needed to stop Simon as soon as possible and get these monsters back to their home world. What if the military came in and tried to hurt the monsters? What if other people started using real weapons? With the monsters attacking back, what would happen?

"We need to get out of this area and find ourselves a restaurant that isn't occupied by these creatures," Sarika said.

"That works for me," Lucas replied. "Hey, Jacob, come on, let's go."

Finding food in Tokyo would likely have been easy, but at the moment a major transformation was taking over the city. For one, people were still recovering from the terrible attack that had happened because of Simon.

Creatures floated around and walked through the streets. At one of the coffee shops, the windows were broken and a tall creature in a black robe and with a face like a deer with antlers and all sat staring at a massive donut.

"Creepy," Sarika said.

"And kinda cool, you have to admit," Lucas replied, earning a grin from her.

They all jogged through the streets where the fog had been not long ago. At a corner where three streets came together and next to a statue of a plump raccoon, they found a ramen shop with an old man who welcomed them with a bow and said, "*Irrashaimase.*"

His eyes focused on Ralli and then Sarika as he said, "You all look like you're not from around here," in broken English.

"That seems to be the norm over the last few minutes," Ralli said. "What's good?"

The man gestured to the wall of pictures of ramen dishes, and Madison selected one that looked spicy and delicious. The picture depicted ramen bowls with a rich brown sauce and chunks of meat. Some had vegetables and eggs, and others had things Madison didn't recognize.

"Holy fluffy monsters, this soup is delicious!" Ralli said.

"Madison, you're not eating," Lucas noted, eyeing her as he slurped noodles noisily.

"Can you eat less like a child?" Madison asked.

"Actually, it's good manners here to slurp noisily," Lucas replied. "Read about it."

Madison had never learned to use chopsticks, so she stuck with the soup spoon. She eyed the bowl uncertainly before taking a sip. Ralli was right. It was amazing, with a thick flavor that was nothing like the boring microwavable ramen back home. Soon she was digging in and even doing her best to slurp up noodles. This was one of the most delicious meals she'd ever had. With each slurp of steaming soup, she could almost forget about the parade of monsters outside or the recent, life-threatening fights.

11

LUCAS

Lucas turned in his seat to take a moment to appreciate what he saw outside the little ramen shop. As a longtime card collector, especially of the type of cards used in battling and monster collecting, he was starting to wish the world could go on like this forever.

A creature like a floating mermaid with three tails floated through the air, holding hands with a birdman with lightning flashing in his eyes. The two circled, and other monsters that resembled fiery monkeys laughed and clapped. One little yellow, dinosaur-like creature appeared at the window of the ramen shop, licked the glass, and then let out a loud burp that caused the glass to shake.

Lucas laughed at that, and Jacob snorted his ramen.

"Gross!" Madison said, pointing at Jacob and the noodle that stuck out of his nose.

"Ack, how's that even possible!" Lucas had to put a hand over his mouth to keep from gagging at the sight that was both humorous and disgusting.

Jacob blushed, breathed in deeply, and the noodle vanished. He gagged, and then it was gone. With a slap of his knee, he pointed at the monsters outside. "This is the best day of my life."

"Don't forget we're not out of danger yet."

As if to highlight her point, a large wolf with glowing horns on its head ran into view, sniffed the air, and then turned to look at them.

Lucas gave the creature a subtle wave with his left hand, his right hand setting down his chopsticks in case he needed to fight.

"Not that one," Ralli said, a hand on his shoulder. "We'll see plenty of scary monsters, but that doesn't mean they pose a threat. It's like people in your world—or... apples. Sometimes there's a bad apple, but you can't tell just by looking at it. Got that from one of your children's books."

"I like it," Madison said.

Easter and Fido had been eating while sitting on

the floor, and the former looked up and said, "Yeah. I mean, I'm starting to look very scary, but I'm super nice, don't you think?"

"Well..." Lucas wasn't sure how to answer that. Easter was a great help to his sister but hadn't spent enough time with all of them just hanging out for Lucas to really know if she was nice.

"You are very handsome today," Easter said and then winked. "See, aren't I nice?"

Lucas laughed, then nodded. "Extremely."

He turned his attention to a trio of tall, blue creatures that looked like aliens. He was humored by the thought because, in a way, weren't all of the creatures out there aliens? If indeed they were from other worlds and dimensions, not just videogame creatures come to life—though it seemed the truth was a bit of both, or all-encompassing.

"Imagine a world where you see people posting about those creatures walking around in the forests or taking dips in our pools," Lucas said with a laugh.

"How do we know which ones are safe?" Madison sipped her soup, watching Ralli over the edge of her bowl.

Ralli cocked her head. "Depends, yeah. Most worlds are actually less violent than I understand

Earth to be, but if they are pushed... they'll push back."

"Let's hope the military or some militia or whatever doesn't come in swinging then," Lucas said. He pulled his bowl over and took a nice slurp of noodles.

The old man was at his kitchen, giving them no mind. He didn't even seem to notice or care that a parade of monsters had started outside. Madison turned to watch, enjoying the warmth in her belly as much as the silly dance of several tall, thin monsters with pink fur. More monsters filed by, some with horns, others looking like massive eyeballs or strange shapes she couldn't begin to understand.

"Where are they going?" Sarika asked.

"My guess," Ralli replied between gulps of soup, the bowl held up to her mouth, "they're on their way to find the closest park, where they'll set up and have a party. Trust me, creatures like this *love* to party."

"Maybe we should join them?" Jacob pushed his empty bowl away.

"As fun as that'd be," Madison interjected, "don't forget that we still have Simon to deal with."

"She's right." Ralli stood and gave the old man a bow, followed by, "*Gotchisosamadeshita!*"

"Wha..." Jacob asked.

"It means something like thank you for the feast," Lucas said and followed suit. The rest did the same, though their attempts sounded more like, "*Go chiso mama Shita.*" Yeah, way off.

Madison looked up from the menu with panic in her eyes and leaned over to Jacob. "We have to figure out a way to pay for this."

He laughed, remembering the loot from defeating the Puppet Master. With a smile, he reached into his pocket and pulled out a handful of coins. "Will this do?"

The old man waved his hand. "No need. No need. We're all in the same situation with the monsters outside. No point in bothering with payment."

Still, they insisted. The old man bowed, and the kids headed for the doors. Before they reached them, Lucas slowed and nudged Jacob.

"You were serious back there?" he asked. "About baseball, not trying to avoid me?"

"Come on man, this is the best! You know I love gaming with you, but I have other interests too. Maybe you could try out for the team?"

Lucas laughed at that, shaking his head. "Nah, I'm good. Not my style."

"Well then..." Jacob shrugged. "Tell you what, I'll make a better effort to do both. Cool? And for now... "Let's join them in the parade."

For a second Lucas was going to reject the idea, but he saw Sarika's eyes light up, and as she stepped out to join the creatures, he couldn't help but be swept up with the idea.

"Well then, hurry up!" he said to Jacob, skipping forward to Sarika's side and laughing as several monkey-like creatures with fiery hair did a dance. She tried to follow along. They waved their hands in the air, shaking one foot and then the other, before they spun around. It was something like the hokey pokey with a bit of the macarena.

Sarika laughed at Lucas attempting to dance, but he kept at it, not caring how ridiculous it made him look.

A gust of wind caught them, and before he knew what was happening, the two were in the air, floating around each other with streams of purple and yellow light.

"What's happening?" Sarika asked with a wide smile.

"I don't know, but it's awesome!"

Lucas put out his arms and spiraled. Then he saw the white wish dragon—a dragon covered in fur that flew through the air without wings—circling them. It met his gaze with wisdom and a flash of playfulness and then moved on and let them back to the ground.

"That was awesome!" Jacob said, joining the parade along with the others and clapping Lucas on the back.

"The fun's just getting started," Fido said at their side, then began chasing his tail.

12

MADISON

Madison followed her brother along the monster parade route, laughing as several others joined in a dance that a group of thin, hairy monsters were leading. Her brother had a point that there was a nice side to all of these creatures being here, even if they did creep her out.

She was eyeing a vending machine and considering trying one of the coffee drinks—after all, she had been awake way too long—when a screech caught her attention.

Spinning to see what was wrong, she first saw only eyes in the darkness of an alley. One second those eyes were there, the next, gone. Not that it would have been anything so strange, considering all of the eyes around here, but this time something in her gut told her there was danger.

"Ralli," Madison said, stepping over to be at her side. "You... good?"

"I sensed it too, yes." Ralli pointed ahead and to the left. "Be careful."

"Actually, I saw something the other way. Eyes watching. It's probably nothing."

"No, if you felt something was off, trust your intuition."

Madison glanced back, alert, ready for anything. "You sure I'm not just being paranoid?"

"Be... ready."

"I'm here with you," Easter said, wings flapping to fly up beside her. You see trouble, point me at 'em, and I'll barbecue the creepo."

"Thanks."

She didn't have to do any pointing, however, because the person behind her sense of unease revealed himself at that exact moment. It started with a gust of wind strong enough to blow Madison sideways so she had to brace herself to not fall. Some of the creatures were blown away while others turned and growled.

All faced a boy who appeared on the balcony of a

building ahead and to the right, in the direction the wind had come from.

"Kraken," Lucas said, and Sarika nodded, both glaring at the boy in a way that told Madison they had met him before.

"And he's not alone," Sarika said, pointing.

Sure enough, past the building and hovering in the sky was a young girl with flowing, blonde hair. With her arms held out, wind whipped out around her. Her face was covered by a blue mask with gold horns. As Madison watched, colors flowed out from the edges of the masks to spread around her and make her take a familiar form. This was the Oni monster Madison had fought in the fog!

"I know that one—Oni... She's a tough cookie." Madison stepped off to the side of the street under cover of a convenience store. She held out her hand and summoned her sword, motioning for the others to join her. "Be ready!"

Lucas eyed her with concern. "So what do we do?"

"I have an idea," Ralli said and then ran off to the crowd of monsters vanishing around the corner.

"Where're you going!" Lucas called after her.

"Just—fight. Keep them occupied!"

Madison shared a worried look with Lucas while Jacob held his ax in the air and shouted up at the twins, "Come down here and fight us!"

"Maybe he shouldn't be goading them on like that," Easter said at Madison's side. She flew over to Fido's side to the left of Madison and Lucas, nudging the dog-looking creature. "Tell him to quiet down, would you?"

"No way. I'm with him!" Fido started barking like a dog, interspersed with challenges like, "*Bark! Bark!* You heard him! Fight! Fight! *Bark! Fight!*"

"If you say so," Kraken replied.

A flash of light flew out around the boy, and energy shot out to surround him in a way that helped Madison understand where he got his name. It formed the shape of a massive sea monster, like the Kraken of mythology—most likely pulling on energy from another world in the metaverse. But it wasn't just a sea monster. As he moved, its fins did too, sending waves of energy blasts down at Madison and her friends.

"Get back!" Ralli shouted and charged in for an attack. She was in bear form, her arms crossed to block the strikes as an energy shield formed in front of her. Each strike sent her back and made the shield shrink, but it was enough to get the others out on the attack.

Lucas was sending mobile lava strikes from his sword, Sarika doing the same with one of her blasters, and Easter flew up to try sending an arrow at the enemy.

"How do we fight something like that?" Madison asked, darting around those energy waves and ducking behind a car that shook when hit.

Easter was at her side, bow and arrow ready. "Same way we do all monsters—as a team."

Madison gave her little friend a nod and then pushed herself up between energy waves. Eyeing a rooftop nearby, she timed it just right to Shadow Move to it and then leaped with a shadow strike for Kraken. To her relief, the strike hit!

He roared, spinning, and she was flung into the air, arms flailing.

"Not good, not good!" she shouted but was relieved to find Easter flying up to her. Easter caught Madison by the back of her shirt and, while not strong enough to fly with her, flapped those little wings to slow the fall enough that she could land in a run and not get hurt. Together, they turned to see Kraken circling Oni. Green, flowing light emerged from the girl to circle her brother, sparkling light flowing from her to where Madison had struck.

"She's healing him!" Lucas said, running to Madison's side. "Same thing's been happening with my lava strikes, and my mana's running low."

"Same!" Jacob said, who also shrugged. "And... I haven't exactly been upgrading projectiles. I don't know how to get up there and help!"

At that moment, both Oni and Kraken turned on them and sent a barrage of attacks.

"Down!" Fido said in a half bark and then tackled Jacob out of the way. With another bark, an energy shield rose up to surround Jacob and then more for the others. The dog creature looked confused. "How..."

"Gave you a nice little upgrade," Jacob said with a grin. "Figured since Easter provides ranged attacks, your specialty can be shields and amplification skills."

"I like it!"

"Over here!" Ralli shouted.

All converged on her at a point behind a small tree and next to the subway station. Madison ducked down behind the subway stop next to Lucas, noting that Ralli set up an energy wall. Blast after blast hit it while the group huddled to figure out a strategy.

"We have to find a way to stop them!" Lucas shouted. "What's giving them such power?"

"The mask!" Ralli replied, on one knee and nearly spent, only one arm still in bear form with those long claws.

"What do you mean?"

"I recognize its code and signature." She threw her arm up to shield them from a blast of blue energy that Kraken sent at them. "That mask was a gift from Simon without a doubt. More than that, I think it holds some of the power of one of those core crystals—as if he's broken one up and embedded it within, so she's able to steal powers from other worlds as long as she wears the mask."

"But there's no way we can reach them!" Madison said, craning her neck to see that Kraken was guarding his sister. Ducking back to avoid another blast, Madison felt a chill run down her spine. "Anyone have any great ideas?"

"Actually, this might help..." Sarika held out her hand so that her hover snowboard appeared. She held it out to Madison. "I don't think I could land the hit, but if you ride, the rest of us could cause a distraction down below."

"And you wouldn't be alone up there," Easter said, burping up a little fireball.

"Whoa, nice!" Madison said with a high five to the dragon creature. "You're doing fire now?"

"Looks like it!"

Madison accepted the snowboard from Sarika, her eyes wide with the idea of flying around in the air on this thing. "Maybe someone else could do this part? Lucas?"

He scoffed, waving the comment off. "With your Shadow Moves, you're definitely the best for this type of surgical strike."

"Surgical?" She arched an eyebrow and then lowered the snowboard so it hovered a couple of inches off the ground. "Whatever."

"We're doing it?" Easter asked, excitedly.

"You bet your sweet wings we are." Madison stepped onto the board with first one foot, then the other. Once she had her balance, she asked, "How's it work?"

"Great thing about it," Sarika said, "just lean left or right to go those directions, while up and down are controlled partially by you moving your feet up or down, but largely by your will, which works out well for me. It's synched with you when riding it, so... you got this!"

"Well then, here goes!"

Madison took a deep breath, about to ride off, but felt a tug on her pant leg.

"Wait," Jacob said. "We're going to cause the distraction. Remember?"

"Ah, got it." Madison almost laughed as the tension left. Then again, it returned nearly as fast when she turned to watch her brother and the others go charging out for round two. Only Easter remained.

"I'll fly to the other side to draw their attention that way even when in the air," Easter said. "Cool?"

"Very cool," Madison replied. She counted to three after Easter had taken off before darting out herself.

She rounded the corner to see chaos. Lucas had summoned his glowing blue wolves and even jumped onto the back of one, riding it up what looked like energy shields that acted as little platforms. Nice moves, but likely to eat up a lot of mana. Jacob was trying to distract the enemy by running around with Fido and making a lot of noise while Sarika and now Easter sent projectiles up.

"Here goes everything!" Madison mumbled to herself and then shot forward on that hovering snowboard.

If the evil twins hadn't been fighting them, this would have been an amazing rush. As it was, Madison bent her knees, hair whipping about her face and behind her with her massive sword glowing brightly. She pulled down her goggles to cover her eyes and then gripped her blade with two hands, ready.

She went straight for the twins, but a stream of red-light-like curtains pulled in front of her, causing the board to stop as if it had slammed into a wall. Jolted and confused, Madison found herself tumbling toward the ground.

"Focus!" Sarika called up from below.

Madison shook her head, held her hands out, and turned her attention back to the enemy. Sure enough, the board righted itself, and she was ascending again. How was she going to ensure the same attack didn't stop her this time? The words Easter had said came back into her mind—about working as a team—so she shouted, "Everyone, attack... *Now!*"

Her friends unleashed, and this time although the red light appeared, it flickered, and Madison was able to pass through. She focused her momentum on reaching Oni since that was the healer of the two, but no matter how fast she flew or how hard she turned, the girl with her stupid mask was faster.

"I can't catch her!" Madison protested, circling around Oni, Easter at her side and sending fireballs at the enemy.

"You have to!" Easter replied. "For your brother!"

Madison glanced down to see that the colorful lights from Oni's robe had Lucas held up like a puppet, one starting to wrap around his neck. He wouldn't be able to fight them off, and in that moment, she was back to a playground when he had been at most six, two bullies trying to pick on him.

She had charged the boys, each about her age, and slammed the first into the ground before pummeling him with two punches and then rolling away from a kick by the second. When she had finished with them, they told everyone around not to mess with her or her brother.

Just like that day, she was determined to be the hero her baby brother needed. She tilted the board to where she was nearly horizontal, flew in with her sword at the ready, and then used the last of her mana to shadow strike. The attack from Kraken below nearly connected with her right elbow, the attack from Oni above sent scrapes along her right side and left tears at the bottom of her shirt. But that didn't matter because she was close enough and had her sword lifted, ready.

That last strike connected, slamming into the Oni mask and splitting it in two. Suddenly the wind stopped. As leaves and debris fell to the ground, so too did the girl collapse. She landed with a thud.

A split second later, her brother was at her side, lifting her. "No, no..." He cradled her, pushing the broken mask aside. Underneath was a pretty girl with freckles on her nose and cheeks and thick eyebrows. Her eyes were closed at first, but as he held her, she coughed and then opened her piercing-blue eyes. Only a bit at first, but then she smiled.

"Let's get out of here," she muttered.

Kraken let out a sob, holding his sister. He turned his attention to Madison and the others. "This won't be the last of us. I'm telling Simon about this, and wherever you go, he'll be ready for you."

He reached into his pocket with the hand that wasn't holding his sister, activated something, and then a red light flashed around them. The light encircled the siblings, flashed brightly, and then vanished—them with it.

"Where'd they go?" Jacob asked, his head spinning.

"To Simon, clearly," Ralli replied.

Madison looked up to see that the parade of monsters was coming to an end. A mix of a dragon and lion creatures made up the end of it, and then the creatures were gone from sight.

"I need a moment," Madison said, wanting to catch her breath. Not sure how to distract herself, she pulled up her screen to finish applying her skill points.

She applied her first point to "Dragonize Pet" and looked forward to seeing the effects of that. Next, she applied a point to "Saddle Summon." Getting two points with level ups sure felt nice!

"No more delays," Madison said and then turned to Ralli. "We have to find the third core. Right?"

"Yes, that's correct," Ralli said. "And it's likely to be well-defended. We need to figure out how to locate it."

"Before you go, can I point out how amazing this is," Jacob said.

"What do you mean?" Madison asked.

"Look at those monsters. It's like something out of a Miyazaki film."

"Yeah, I feel like we could see Totoro waiting for a bus with an umbrella in the corner." They all laughed at the idea.

"We should go to the internet café," Ralli said, indicating a building across the street. "With some triangulation, I think we should be able to locate the final source of the monsters."

Madison agreed that Easter and Fido would hide since she could summon them with the key again when needed. Then she followed Ralli and the others into the tall building with the internet café sign.

13

LUCAS

Walking into the internet café, Lucas was amazed to see a room full of various walled-off areas for people to use computers, VR, and more. One had a door open that even showed a foldout couch for sleeping. A soda machine to the right of the entrance said, "Free refills" beneath some Japanese he couldn't read.

"I'll get on a computer and start looking for the most concentrated areas of monsters and the like," Ralli said but then froze with a look of confusion.

"What is it?" Lucas asked.

"Just that I'm not sure I know how to use a computer in your world. Not without my weird access skills that would likely draw too much attention our way."

"I got you," Madison said, and the two went arm in arm to one of the closed-in booths.

"And us?" Lucas asked.

Madison grinned over her shoulder. "Get to know each other better?"

"And don't forget to use the potty, hydrate, you know—all those weird things humans do."

"Ralli!" Madison hissed.

Lucas wanted to face palm, but he glanced around and realized nobody had noticed the strange comment. Either they didn't speak English or, more likely, they were too polite to show it. She wasn't wrong, though. Some liquid and a quick bathroom break were exactly what he needed.

First things first, he asked, "Sarika, can I get you something?"

"Juice?"

"Of course." He went to the drink bar and saw Calpisu and other strange drinks but opted for simple apple juice for both of them.

He turned to bring it to her where she sat at a row of chairs nearby, but Jacob stood in his way, grinning.

"So…" Jacob asked.

"What?"

He lowered his voice. "You and Sarika spent a good amount of time alone. I'm sensing a little crush."

"Shut up." Lucas almost wanted to throw his juice on his friend but instead side-stepped him and whispered, "We were too busy fighting monsters to even think about it."

Jacob scoffed but let it go as he went to grab a soda.

Lucas handed over the juice to Sarika but turned away as he took a sip of his own. Somehow, after Jacob's comments about having a crush, he felt awkward next to her.

"You feeling okay?" she asked.

"Just... nervous about all the monsters."

She stepped around to be in his line of sight, giving him a little wave. "Hello, Earth to Lucas. It's fun, remember? We set them free."

"But..." He was about to argue that the monsters he would be afraid of were the ones they were searching for to fight. Except, that would make him look like a coward, and he wasn't really scared of fighting them. If anything, he was actually excited to go fight them. After all, it was better than dealing with this awkward situation!

"But..." Sarika asked but then just laughed. "Lucas, you're being really weird. So how about this – I'm going to help the girls while you and your buddy Jacob look over your level upgrades and skill trees there."

"Sure. Er, have fun."

Her advice was actually a great idea! He had been looking forward to applying his skill points, but he had gotten carried away with all that was happening. Now he really wanted to get to work on upgrades but had a serious need to use the bathroom.

Judging by the dance Jacob was doing, he had the same thought.

"Don't follow me to the toilet," Jacob said as the two started down the hall.

"Give me a break," Lucas replied.

They quickly took care of business and then moved to another of the internet booths for privacy.

"Whoa, they have all kinds of games," Lucas said, checking out the screen.

"Not why we're here though. Is it?" Jacob reclined on a cushioned bench and pulled up his screen, so Lucas did the same.

He eyed his screen and the Beastmaster skill tree. So far, he had the Summon Wolves skill and riding ability, and next he could upgrade the wolves to make them into dire wolves. That sounded cool, so he went ahead with the upgrade and was excited to see it, so he added a bonus "Stunning Howl" that would allow him to stun enemies. For now, he didn't upgrade his sword's Volcanic Path but might come back to that in the future.

"Not bad," he said, closing the screen and turning to Jacob. "Did you get anything cool?"

Jacob grinned, pulling up his sleeve and then flexing. To Lucas's surprise, his best friend had muscles popping up that had never been there before.

"What..." Lucas started.

"I put all my emphasis on strength, my skill points to the Barbarian class."

"Nice!"

"Double nice," a girl said, walking by and giving him a smile.

Jacob's cheeks went red, his mouth hanging open.

"Maybe we should keep it down about the upgrades when in public," Lucas said. "Although it clearly has its benefits."

Both turned to see the girl giggling with her

friends before turning a corner and disappearing from sight.

"Lucas?" Sarika's voice carried over the walls of the booths. "Where'd you go?"

"Over here," he said, standing to head out to her.

"Your girlfriend is calling you," Jacob whispered with a wink.

"Dude..." Lucas shook his head, deciding it was better to ignore the comment. He opened the small, swinging door and nearly walked right into her.

"Oh, hey." She brushed her dark hair behind her ear, looking up at him from her wheelchair. "We're ready to go. You?"

"Yeah. Ralli found the third location? Is it close?"

She laughed. "Not exactly, but still in this part of the world."

"And that is..."

"Okinawa. It's an island with—"

"A lot of military bases, right? Yeah, Grandpa was stationed there and used to talk about it all the time. The beaches, the caves..."

"Well, looks like we're going to get a chance to see the island, but this won't exactly be a sightseeing trip."

"How do we get there?" Jacob asked, leaning over

the shoulder-high wall that separated them from the booth.

"Digitally," Sarika said with a grin and then turned to Ralli and Madison as the two stepped up to join. "Isn't that right, Ralli?"

"I have a connection established. Come on, everyone in here." Ralli motioned and led the way with Madison back to the cramped internet booth they had been using.

She woke the computer from sleep mode, but Lucas leaned in, noting a glowing folder that appeared and said, "To Lucas and Madison" as the title.

"Wait, what's that?" he asked.

"Interesting," Madison said, taking over from Ralli to click on the folder. Within was a password-protected video.

"Got it," Lucas said, and leaned over to type in first his sister's birthday, then his own. Of course it worked. His mom used that for everything. It was a video of their mom, clearly in a vehicle and on the road, with Driana in the background.

"Your friend found me," their mom started. "It's all a bit much to process, but I've seen the news and can't deny that strange things are happening to our world. I want you both to know that I love you very much and that I'm safe. We're going off the grid, so don't worry about us. I would tell you both to stay safe, too, but... I understand that what you're doing is beyond that. So instead, I'll simply tell you to stay healthy. Look out for each other. Make that Simon jerk pay."

With a kiss to the screen, she signed off. Lucas and Madison shared a look of relief. Knowing their mom was safe with Driana would make the next phase of this fight that much easier to stomach.

No sooner had the video closed than the entire building started to shake! Bags of chips and many flavors of KitKats fell off a shelf, drinks spilled, and the lights above swayed.

"*Ahhh!*" Jacob shouted.

Lucas braced himself, caught even more off guard as Sarika's wheelchair rolled and she had to catch herself on his arm before locking her wheels in place. She didn't let go even after the shaking stopped.

"That was crazy!" Madison said.

Sarika nodded, slowly loosening her grip on his arm. "Sorry, I... I'm not used earthquakes."

"Japan supposedly has them often," Lucas replied, not sure what to say.

"I don't think it was an earthquake," Ralli said,

turning and motioning for them to hurry. "Not a normal one, anyway. I think he knows we're coming... and he's scared."

The End

———

AUTHOR NOTES

THANK you for reading *Invaded by Videogames*, Metaverse Legends Book 3! I hope you enjoyed it as much as I enjoyed writing it.

This third book explored the growth of our beloved siblings and their friends as they faced even greater challenges in their fight against evil.

Writing this story was a thrilling and challenging experience. I wanted to create a vivid and immersive experience for my readers, transporting them to the bustling streets of Tokyo, Japan, while maintaining the essence of what made the Metaverse Chronicles so special. Having lived in Japan myself, I drew upon my personal experiences and memories to bring the setting and culture to life with authenticity and accuracy.

Throughout the book, you may have noticed the

theme of unity and trust being tested. Our heroes had to learn to rely on each other and their newfound allies to overcome the various obstacles and dangers they encountered. It was important for me to delve deeper into the emotional journey of each character, exploring the complexities of their relationships and individual struggles.

I also wanted to challenge the preconceived notions of what a "monster" is. "Real World Invasion" blurred the lines between good and evil, showing that not all threats come in the form of terrifying creatures and that even those who seem monstrous can possess a hidden depth and humanity.

As always, I hope you enjoyed reading this book as much as I enjoyed writing it. It is my sincerest wish that you found inspiration, excitement, and perhaps even a little bit of yourself within its pages.

Thank you for joining Lucas, Madison, and their friends on this incredible adventure. Your support means the world to me, and I couldn't wait to bring you more thrilling stories from the Metaverse Chronicles.

Thank you for joining me on this journey!

. . .

Best,
Justin

———

Please leave a review, and find more of my books on Amazon and in KU:

www.amazon.com/Justin-M-Stone/e/
B088DKW86R

ABOUT THE AUTHOR

Justin M. Stone is a novelist (*Allie Strom and the Ring of Solomon; Falls of Redemption*), videogame writer (*Game of Thrones; Walking Dead; Michonne*), podcaster, and screenwriter. He has written about taking writing from hobby to career in his book *Creative Writing Career* and its sequel, and how veterans can pursue their passions in *Military Veterans in Creative Careers*. Justin studied writing at Johns Hopkins University.

———

To receive other free stories and audiobooks, as well as future updates, sign up for Justin's newsletter.
bit.ly/JustinMStone
And join my Facebook Group!
www.facebook.com/groups/JustinMStone

Printed in Great Britain
by Amazon

32622345R00086